$1.50

S0-AVX-315

PINNED DOWN IN A DEADLY RAIN OF INDIAN GUN FIRE!

In the shallow depression some fifty yards behind him, Colonel Marcus Cavanaugh heard the moans of wounded men begging for water.

"We need water and ammunition, Colonel," Captain Lemaster pointed out.

"I'm aware of that, Captain."

A soft thud sounded next to Marcus as an Indian bullet dug into the sandy soil less than a foot away. The river was close but getting to it would not be easy, with the entire distance covered by hostile gun fire. On the right end of the perimeter, an A Company trooper cried out and pitched forward, yet another casualty.

Marcus gritted his teeth. "Captain, what we've got to do is dig in and hang on 'til we can get out of here after dark. Or there won't be much need for either water or ammunition."

"It's going to be a long day, Colonel," Lemaster said, shaking his head.

"It will be at that," Marcus agreed grimly. "But I'm open to suggestions, Captain . . . "

**Look for all the books in
the ARROW AND SABER series:**

BATTLE OF
HORSETOOTH MOUNTAIN
G.A. CARRINGTON

A DELL BOOK

Special thanks to Jerry Keenan

Published by
Dell Publishing
a division of Bantam Doubleday Dell
Publishing Group, Inc.
666 Fifth Avenue
New York, New York 10103

ISBN: 0-440-20384-8

Printed in the United States of America
Published simultaneously in Canada

June 1990

10 9 8 7 6 5 4 3 2 1

OPM

For my children, Kelly and Andy,
with much love.

Chapter One

The village stretched for nearly a mile along the banks of the river, some two hundred tipis standing sleepily in the smoky blue haze of the late summer afternoon. The villagers went about their business slowly, without spirit. Almost without exception, they had the drawn look of a defeated people.

Chief Michael Bright Sky walked slowly along the river, pausing now and then to look at the shallow waters, pondering the plight of his people, whose situation worsened with each day. Promises pledged to the Nez Perce Indians in the treaty with the white men had not been kept. The people were hungry, and seldom smiled anymore. Bright Sky yearned for the exuberance of village life he had known as a boy when the buffalo were many.

He turned and walked back to his lodge. Entering, he sat down and watched his wife, Swan, cooking over a small fire. Tall and willowy, with silky, jet black hair, Swan remained an attractive woman, who, despite her

1

approaching middle years moved as sinuously now as any female half her age. Yet it was Swan's tremendous inner strength that Bright Sky had come to appreciate as her most enduring quality. He barely noticed the tipi flap open. Three men entered and seated themselves across the fire from him. They said nothing as Swan silently handed each a bowl of food.

"I am sorry we have not more to offer," Bright Sky said.

The one on the left, an elder known as Elk, waved the apology aside with a toothless grin. "In my case, it matters little anymore."

The others smiled at this, but grew quickly serious again.

"We know you are deeply troubled," Owl, the middle member began, "but the time has come for us to act."

Bright Sky studied him. "And what would you have us do, Owl?"

The three visitors glanced at each other, and then the third member of the trio, Black Dove responded, leaning forward slightly to lend emphasis to his words.

"We must leave this place."

For a long moment Bright Sky said nothing, staring at the fire. He had known it would come to this, and he struggled against an urge to agree.

"No," he responded at length, shaking his head. "We have given our word to live according to the treaty."

"And what of the white man's word," Owl retorted angrily, gesturing with his free hand. "What of the spoiled beef and moldy flour? Has the white man kept his word to us?"

Elk nodded. "And our land. They keep taking more and more. Soon there will be no place for us."

"Now they say we can no longer travel over the mountains to hunt buffalo," Black Dove added.

"I understand all of these things," Bright Sky said earnestly. "But we must be patient, my friends. One day things will be better for us."

The trio looked at one another. Sensing Bright Sky's determination, they knew it was pointless to pursue the issue further.

Suddenly the sound of a commotion outside caught everybody's attention. With Bright Sky in the lead, they all went outside.

Villagers were crowding about two warriors who rode slowly through the village, leading a horse. Across its back lay an inert boy, his hands dangling limply beneath its belly.

Halting in front of Bright Sky, the brave called Blue Water dismounted. Gravely, he handed the reins of the riderless horse to Bright Sky. Suddenly devastated, Bright Sky recognized the body of Young Hawk, his son. Swan gasped, then moaned softly.

Two warriors removed the body and gently laid it on the ground. Dropping to her knees, Swan began to keen softly. She placed her hands tenderly on the cheeks of her son's youthful face, which now bore the ashen pallor of death.

Bright Sky looked on in numb disbelief. "Only a boy of fifteen summers," he muttered.

"The rancher's men hanged him in a tree," Blue Water announced grimly. "For stealing a crippled cow."

"He was hungry," Bright Sky said simply.

"But they have paid for it," Blue Water declared defiantly. "We killed one of their young men. Now they, too, have somebody to mourn!"

Bright Sky looked at the two men who had brought

him the body of his son. He had felt a rage he had not imagined himself capable of feeling, and now, on the heels of Blue Water's pronouncement, he felt a new adversary, fear—of the reprisal he knew was certain to follow.

"We must prepare for the ceremony," he announced softly, placing his hand gently on Swan's shoulder. Bending down, he picked up the lifeless form, and cradled it in his arms. He carried it into the tipi, laying the body gently in the bed that would claim it for the last time.

Feeling the need to be alone, he left the tipi and returned to the shallow river. He was barely conscious of the eyes that watched him, sharing his grief. It was not until the shadows of afternoon began to lengthen that he left the river and returned to his lodge. He eased down in front of the fire and forced himself to look beyond his own grief to the needs of the people.

Blue Water's revenge on the rancher's men would not be ignored by the white men and his people would suffer the consequences. Yet it was inevitable. He had been wrong to imagine they could abide by the treaty and still survive. How long could people live without food, without the freedom to roam the great prairies in search of the buffalo? Perhaps Owl was right. Perhaps it was time to leave while his people still had the strength to do so.

Bright Sky became conscious of Swan at his side. She added wood to the fire, and as though privileged to know his thoughts, asked softly, "When will we leave this place?"

Bright Sky remained silent for so long Swan thought perhaps he had chosen not to answer.

"We will leave after the ceremony," he said, finally.

4

"The bones of our son willl remain here, in the land of the Nez Perce forever."

He got to his feet. "I will summon the others so we can make plans. There is much to talk of."

That night six braves, Bright Sky, Owl, Elk, Black Dove, Stone Bear and Little Raven, gathered in a council. A strikingly handsome man with piercing black eyes, Little Raven, given the Christian name of Paul at an agency school many years ago, was a warrior of great repute. Although five summers younger than his brother, Bright Sky, he was taller.

"It is agreed, then," Bright Sky said, recapping their discussion. "We will go to the Grandmother Land in the north where the Sioux went after the fight with the Yellow Hair. First, we move south over the mountains and through Lobo Canyon. From there we turn east, cross the Firehole River and head through the land of the stinking springs, then north to Horsetooth Mountain. From there it is only two sleeps to the Grandmother Land."

"A long journey, Bright Sky," Elk said softly.

Bright Sky nodded. "But one we must undertake. I don't see that there is any choice for us. Winter will come soon. If we do not go now, we will starve." He glanced around and saw the nods of affirmation. "We leave here at first light the day after tomorrow." The Nez Perce chief stood, signalling that the council was over.

Raven remained a moment after the others left.

"A difficult choice, my brother, but a strong one." He grasped Bright Sky by the upper arm. "We will succeed."

A grim smile crossed Bright Sky's mouth. "I pray you are right, Raven, for I fear our people may pay a terrible price."

Chapter Two

Second Lieutenant Francis Xavier Banning, West Point, Class of '83, raised his right arm to signal a halt. Behind him the twelve-man detachment from Company A, Eleventh Cavalry reined their mounts to a halt, happy for a pause, however brief. The early September day was young but pregnant with heat. Even in the shadow of the heavily timbered slopes of the lush valley the heat was oppressive.

Beside Lieutenant Banning a leather-faced man, Sergeant Greer, studied the Nez Perce camp beyond the bend of the small stream. He spat a thin stream of tobacco juice to one side.

"There she sits, Lieutenant," he observed dryly. "I expect the pair we're after are in there somewhere, and feelin' mighty comfortable right about now."

"Let's hope they stay put long enough for us to interrupt their comfort, Sergeant."

Greer, a veteran of nineteen years, glanced at the red-headed young lieutenant. He had little respect for most officers, particularly the ones who seemed adept at making fools of themselves. This one was a kid, with a mouth to match the color of his hair. He wished the colonel had assigned a more experienced officer, but that was the colonel's business and regimental commanders did not ordinarily consult with sergeants on such matters.

Lieutenant Banning removed his blue kepi and wiped the perspiration from his forehead and the back of his neck. He motioned the unit forward with a downward gesture of his right arm. The detail moved ahead, the shod hooves of their mounts clattering on the rocks of the stream bed.

This was his first independent assignment and Banning was anxious to do well. He hoped the sergeant hadn't detected the nervousness he felt. Nothing at the Point had quite prepared him for what he was about to do—arrest two Indians for theft and murder. When it came to military matters he felt confident enough, but this was police work and it left him with an uncomfortable feeling. Nevertheless, orders were orders and an officer had to expect the unexpected.

As the detachment neared the Nez Perce camp, one of the village curs dashed out, barking furiously and darting in and out among the horses. The troopers cursed and hauled back on the reins to maintain control.

Entering the village, Banning was conscious of hostile stares from the villagers. Undoubtedly, they knew why he had come, and dealing with them would not be easy. He found himself hoping the sergeant would have a sense of what to do and immediately was angry with himself for his own lack of confidence.

"That's Bright Sky, Lieutenant," Greer said to him, pointing. "The one up ahead there on the left . . ."

"Thank you, Sergeant," Banning offered crisply. "When we stop I will do the talking unless I ask your opinion, specifically, is that clear?" His voice exuded the kind of assurance that left no doubt as to who was in command. What he failed to observe was the disdain in the eyes of his sergeant.

Banning halted the detachment and looked down at the Indian called Michael Bright Sky. The Nez Perce chief did not have a commanding physical appearance, but rather a sense of presence and dignity. "I am Lieutenant Banning from Fort Casey. I am here to arrest two of your people."

"I understand why you are here, Lieutenant," Bright Sky said in nearly perfect English. "I have been expecting you. Please come inside," he said, gesturing to his tipi. "It will be best to talk of the matter in my lodge."

Banning glanced about uncomfortably. The sergeant wore a non- committal expression. Banning had been prepared for resistance, not hospitality. Hospitality made him suspicious. Still, he had no reason to expect treachery. At Fort Casey, Colonel Cavanaugh had spoken highly of this man and the colonel must know. Banning nodded, swung down from the saddle, and followed Bright Sky into the tipi.

The interior was surprisingly cool. Bright Sky motioned him to sit. A squaw appeared and set in front of him a bowl of what appeared to be chunks of meat in a thick sauce.

"Now, Lieutenant," Bright Sky began. "Which of my warriors do you wish to arrest?" He dipped his fingers into the bowl and withdrew a chunk of meat.

Banning followed the example of his host, grasping a chunk of meat with his fingers and putting it in his mouth. The flavor was somewhat sweet.

8

"I am here to arrest Blue Water and Touch-the-Sky for murder and stealing."

Bright Sky nodded somberly. "And what will happen to them?"

"They will be tried in a court of law for their crimes," Banning said. "What their punishment might be is not for me to say."

Bright Sky looked at him steadily for a long moment. "I would like to ask you a question, Lieutenant."

Banning nodded. "Of course."

"Have you arrested the men who hanged my son?"

Banning frowned, puzzled.

"The rancher's men. They hanged my son from a tree for taking a crippled cow. He had only seen fifteen summers, Lieutenant. Like all of us, he was hungry because you do not provide us with the things promised in the treaty."

Francis X. Banning squirmed uncomfortably. He was totally unprepared for this, and Michael Bright Sky's eyes bore through him like hot pokers.

"Do you have children, Lieutenant?" Bright Sky asked.

Banning shook his head. "I'm not married."

Bright Sky nodded. "One day you may have a son. If you do, think of him being choked by a rope until his face turns purple while he struggles. Yes, Lieutenant, it is an ugly way to die."

Bright Sky looked down into the fire for a long moment, then back at the ashen-faced young lieutenant. "When you arrest the rancher's men, Lieutenant, then will I turn over Blue Water and Touch-the-Sky to you, but not before."

Banning set his bowl down. "I am sorry about your son. What the rancher's men did was wrong, but what your warriors did was also wrong, and my orders are to arrest Blue Water and Touch-the-Sky. Besides, it doesn't seem to me that your people are all that hungry," he said, motioning to his bowl.

Bright Sky smiled. "Unfortunately, our supply of puppies is small and we are forced to seek meat elsewhere. Surely we cannot depend on Agent Craslow . . . "

Banning felt nauseous. "You mean I've been eating dog?" he said, getting slowly to his feet.

Bright Sky nodded, an amused smile tugging at the corners of his full mouth. "Yes, Lieutenant, but you must admit it is quite good."

Banning looked down at his host, feeling the color rise in his face. He did not appreciate being the victim of Bright Sky's small joke.

"My orders are to arrest Blue Water and Touch-the-Sky. Either you produce them or I will order my men to search the camp."

Bright Sky sighed deeply. "I cannot issue such an order."

"Very well," Banning said, starting outside.

Once outside the tipi, Banning stalked over to Greer. "Sergeant, you will search the village. If the men we are after are here you will place them under arrest."

"Yes, sir." The sergeant saluted casually, turned in the saddle, and sent the detachment moving through the village in pairs.

As the troopers went about their assignment, the inhabitants of the village began to congregate around Banning, their faces sullen and hard. Banning shifted uneasily under their scrutiny. He found himself wishing Colonel Cavanaugh were there.

At the far end of the village a commotion erupted. Presently Sergeant Greer rode up.

"We found 'em, Lieutenant," he reported, ejecting

10

a stream of tobacco juice off to the side. "And if you don't mind my sayin' so, Lieutenant, these folks ain't none too happy 'bout it neither. I suggest we waste no time heading back to Fort Casey."

"I'm well aware of our position, Sergeant," Banning replied, hoping he sounded more confident than he felt.

As the troopers marched the two prisoners forward the mood of the villagers grew ugly. Suddenly, from exactly which direction Banning wasn't certain, a rock struck his mount on the neck, frightening the horse, causing him to pitch and dance. Being a good horseman, Banning was able to check the animal and settle him down.

"You had better instruct your people to behave or we'll be arresting more than these two," he warned Bright Sky.

"Would you arrest an entire village, Lieutenant?"

Banning felt his face coloring, and out of the corner of his eye he thought he detected the hint of a smirk on Greer's face.

"I will arrest anyone who attempts to interfere with us." He looked at Greer.

"Let's be on our way, Sergeant."

Greer nodded and ordered the detachment to form up in twos, with their prisoners mounted and in the middle, hands tied to the saddle.

"These men will be given a fair trial," Banning said, addressing Bright Sky. "Thank you for your hospitality."

Bright Sky nodded briefly, and Banning thought he detected a sense of sadness in the eyes of the Nez Perce leader.

From somewhere in the crowd, a voice expressed defiance. It was followed by a thrown rock, then another and another. Each act of rock throwing was supported by a rising cacophony of angry voices.

Banning was confused. Should he order his men to fight or run?

The soldiers shifted about uncertainly, reflecting the confusion of their leader. A trooper's horse reared. Another blue uniform was struck by a rock. Panicked, one of the troopers fired a shot and a Nez Perce slumped to the ground.

Bright Sky waded into the crowd to restore some semblance of order, but even he, with his forceful presence, was overwhelmed by the emotion of the crowd.

Several villagers grabbed Banning. He struggled to free himself.

"Let's get the hell out of here, Sergeant. Now!" Banning screamed, pulling away from his attackers. Suddenly, Banning felt the splatter of something hot across his face. His composure collapsed when he looked at Sergeant Greer and saw his head cleft in two by a hatchet. Banning wiped the sergeant's brains from his face.

The troopers began firing wildly as the Nez Perce villagers swarmed around them. Having long since lost control of their prisoners, the panic-driven troopers now fought for survival. Events had moved far beyond the ability of any one man to determine their direction. The last thing Banning remembered was the hammer on his Colt falling on an empty chamber as he watched the Nez Perce descend on him and drag him to the ground.

The villagers overwhelmed the detachment. Some troopers were killed in their saddles, while others were dragged to the ground, with only moments to ponder their fates.

Of the twelve troopers that had accompanied Banning into the Nez Perce village, soon only five remained. A corporal named Elias Jones, who somehow managed to rise to the occasion, gathered the surviving troopers and ordered them to fall back, working their Springfields and maintaining at least the semblance of a defensive posture.

The five cavalrymen worked their way steadily back to the crest of the low ridge above the village. Corporal Jones exhorted his men to keep moving while he fired at the closing Nez Perce.

The heavy report of his military issue Springfield mingled with the cries of the villagers as they surged forward. Once his men disappeared down the reverse slope of the ridge, Jones took off after them, leaving the villagers behind. Behind them, the Nez Perce followed, most on foot.

Bright Sky watched, the heaviness of the moment weighing on him. It was only the beginning and he feared to think where the end might lie.

Chapter Three

Colonel Marcus Cavanaugh, commanding officer, Eleventh United States Cavalry Regiment, moved to the center of the room, looking dapper as befitted the occasion of this late summer ball, sponsored by Fort Casey's non-commissioned officers.

Although he had now turned forty, Marcus Cavanaugh's six-foot, one-hundred and eighty pound frame had not yet surrendered to the assault of middle-age flab, thanks to the years spent on one hard field campaign or another. The only visible signs of age were crowsfeet around the eyes and a hint of gray at the temples. Even though he had a wide, full mouth and patrician nose, he was not a strikingly handsome man. Yet there was a certain quality about him that women often found attractive. It was his strength of character that had been forged by self-discipline and dedication to his professional calling.

As was the custom, he approached the wife of the post sergeant-major, bowed and extended his arm, which she accepted gracefully. Together they returned to the center of the room while the regimental band filled the evening with music.

The sergeant-major's wife was an excellent dancer, having participated in many such affairs during her army life. Marcus knew full well that she—and other women like her—was more responsible for the strength of the frontier army's non-commissioned officer corps than most realized.

As they whirled across the floor to the tune of a lively round dance, he couldn't resist stealing a quick glance at Elizabeth Ronayne before she disappeared among the whirl of dancers. He had enjoyed the pleasure of her company this summer and felt a twinge of regret when he realized she would return to the East the day after tomorrow.

Marcus did not ordinarily find himself thinking a great deal about women, or at least about any one woman. The army had been his mistress, and that commitment had left little room for competition. When Elizabeth Ronayne arived at Fort Casey as a summer guest of her sister and brother-in-law, Sally and Timothy Sheehan, it introduced a romantic element into Marcus Cavanaugh's life that he had not had to confront in the past. It had been a pleasant if somewhat unsettling experience.

The dance concluded with the guests politely applauding the regimental band, whose members were perspiring freely from the intensity of their efforts. Marcus bowed slightly to his partner, who curtsied in turn.

"Thank you, Colonel, for a lovely dance."

"My pleasure, ma'am," he replied with a smile. From the corner of his eye, he spotted Elizabeth Ronayne chatting with the post surgeon and his wife. He turned back to the sergeant-major's wife. "If you will excuse me . . ."

"Certainly, Colonel," she smiled, following the direction of Cavanaugh's glance across the room.

Marcus turned and strode over to Elizabeth Ronayne. "I was wondering, Miss Ronayne, if I might have the honor of this dance."

The pretty young woman smiled and nodded briefly. "Why of course, Colonel."

Marcus turned to the surgeon and his wife. "Doctor, Mrs. Grady. If you will excuse us."

He slipped his hand around Elizabeth's waist and they flowed across the floor to the gently swelling strains of "Aura Lee." Halfway through the song he became aware of a commotion at the entrance. A corporal named Jones from A Company was obviously disturbed by something from the way he was talking to the regimental adjutant, Lieutenant John Brandt. Professional instinct warned him that something was wrong.

He excused himself from Elizabeth and went over to the two men. As he approached, Corporal Jones immediately came to attention.

"Stand easy, Corporal," Marcus said.

"Colonel," Lieutenant Brandt started to explain, "the detachment sent to arrest those two Nez Perce warriors ran into trouble. Corporal Jones here reports Lieutenant Banning and five others dead."

Marcus took a deep breath. "What happened, Corporal?"

Jones told the story, the words tumbling out of his mouth in a rush.

"Thank you, Corporal. Good report. That will be all. Get some rest."

"Yes, sir," Jones said, saluting. With a tired about-face he turned and left.

Cavanaugh turned to Lieutenant Brandt. "We've been sitting on a powder keg, John, and somebody's just lit the fuse."

First Lieutenant Johnny Brandt had been with Marcus Cavanaugh for nearly five years now. They were widely separated in both rank and age, but they had similar sensitivities that allowed them to communicate. Brandt understood the colonel's sense of dread.

"Lieutenant, have A and B Companies ready to march in an hour. I'm going out to the reservation. In the meantime, direct Major Damon to hold the rest of the regiment in readiness. Better get off a wire to department headquarters, too. If we're lucky this thing will burn out quickly. If not, well, Abrams had best hear about it now," Marcus said, referring to Brigadier General Carlton Abrams.

He walked to the open window and looked out at a sickle moon hanging in the eastern sky. It reminded him of another night, further back in his memory than he cared to remember.

They had been hunting among the high, remote peaks of the rugged Grizzly Mountains, where the weather seldom seemed to stray far from being cool if not downright cold. He was a young second lieutenant and Michael Bright Sky, who was only slightly older, even then was a respected and influential member of his tribe.

Fresh from West Point, Marcus had been assigned to the Nez Perce agency as part of a small military contingent. He had become acquainted with Michael Bright Sky and taken an immediate liking to him. For his part, Bright Sky sensed a kindred spirit in Marcus Cavanaugh, and the relationship had grown from there.

During the next two years, the pair grew increasingly close in friendship. Bright Sky shared with Marcus the

17

ways of the Nez Perce. Marcus, in turn, explained the intricacies of the white world to Bright Sky.

Their talks took place around a warming fire that thwarted the deep chill of the high Grizzlys and encouraged conversation. On not a few occasions the talks lasted until dawn.

But there was one special time that both would never forget. An early snow storm had caught them by surprise. Seeking shelter, Bright Sky had slipped and fractured a leg. How long he had carried the fallen Indian, Marcus could not remember. Miraculously, he found a cave in which they sought refuge to wait out the fury of the season's first blizzard.

Marcus set the bone, while beads of perspiration stood out on Bright Sky's forehead. It was the most difficult deed Marcus had ever performed, and the memory of the moment was etched forever in his mind. Later, when the little food they had was gone and Marcus began to despair, it was Bright Sky who provided the optimism they needed for survival. Finally the storm passed, and they were able to struggle back down the mountain. By then, a new bond existed between the two men, tempering their relationship in the fierce crucible of a life-threatening experience.

"Shall I accompany, sir?" Brandt asked.

Startled from his thoughts, Marcus glanced at him and flashed a quick smile. "Of course, John. You expect me to take the field without my trusted adjutant?"

Brandt smiled. "Of course not, sir."

"Better see if you can round up Simon, too," Marcus added, referring to Simon Oliver, Fort Casey's chief scout, as much a legend for his bouts with the bottle as for his scouting ability.

"I'll see to it, sir," Brandt replied. He walked over

to the bandstand to make the unpleasant announcement.

Marcus rejoined Elizabeth. "I'm sorry," he said. "I'm afraid I must put an end to the evening, at least for myself."

"A frightful way to end my visit," she declared, pouting. "Trouble . . . ?"

"Some. Difficult to say how bad at this time. May I see you to your quarters?"

She nodded and offered her arm. They stepped out into the nascent coolness of the aging summer evening. Above them a black velvet sky glittered with stars, overpowering the gleam of the thin crescent moon. They walked slowly across the shadow shrouded parade ground.

"Does it look like an uprising?" Elizabeth inquired.

"I hope for the best and fear for the worst," Marcus replied grimly.

They walked on in silence. She sensed his concern and did not intrude.

"I'm sorry," he said presently. "I'm afraid I'm not very good company."

"No apology necessary," she said softly. "It's been a wonderful evening. And a summer I shall never forget, Colonel."

"Marcus," he corrected, adding, "It has been an enjoyable summer for me as well." He sensed her weighing the significance of his offering.

"I hope your return journey is without incident, Miss Ronayne."

"Elizabeth," she corrected softly, at which they both chuckled briefly.

"Do you expect to remain in the West?" she asked after a moment of silence.

"In recent years the idea of a teaching position at the Point has held a certain appeal."

"That would be a considerable change from the life you've known."

"That it would. Somehow, I no longer find the prospect as unexciting as I once did. Perhaps it's time for a change."

"You will know when it is," she observed, in a tone of voice Marcus somehow found encouraging.

Reaching her brother-in-law's quarters, they paused.

"Elizabeth. I would like to call on you, should circumstances ever permit me to be in New York."

"I would be disappointed if you did not."

"Good night, Elizabeth."

She smiled up at Cavanaugh, her blue eyes laughing slightly and a hint of a smile on her full lips. Quickly, she raised herself on her toes and kissed him.

"Good night, Marcus, and take care."

Before he could respond, she was gone. For a moment, Cavanaugh stood still, savoring her kiss, and feeling a rush of euphoria. He was smiling from ear to ear. Then the matter at hand invaded his thoughts.

He turned and walked back across the parade ground toward the lights of the headquarters building, where Johnny Brandt was in the process of organizing their departure. As Marcus pondered the events of the evening he was troubled by a growing sense of uneasiness over the news from the reservation. Five dead soldiers was a serious matter, but he knew it was impossible for his old friend Michael Bright Sky to let such a thing happen. Cavanaugh could only speculate the Nez Perce chief must have been out of the camp. He was duty bound to punish the perpetrators of the murders, and he prayed that the matter would go no further than that.

*　　*　　*

Some hours later, two companies of cavalry rode through the gray light of early dawn, with Marcus Cavanaugh at the head. Behind him, the squeak of saddle leather and the occasional clatter of steel shod hooves on rock barely disturbed the placid September morning.

"What say you, Simon?" Cavanaugh asked, addressing his chief scout.

"'Bout what?" Simon Oliver replied.

"What have we gotten ourselves into, Simon?"

Simon Oliver, riding a sorrel gelding, spat out a thin stream of tobacco juice. "Well you can call it a hunch if you like, Marcus, but I wouldn't make no long range plans if I was you. Not for a while anyway."

Marcus Cavanaugh nodded. "My sentiments exactly, Simon. Any recommendations?"

"Jest let it happen, Marcus. Don't be too quick to jump."

"Wisely put, Simon. Wisely put."

The gray-bearded scout spat again, wiping the overflow from his lips with his elkskin shirt sleeve. "Nothin' more than common sense, Marcus. Nothin' special 'bout it."

Marcus smiled at the scout's straight forward philosophy. Simpler was usually better, but how often it was rejected. He found himself envying Simon Oliver's approach to life.

It was nearing mid-afternoon when they reached the divide that marked the border of the Nez Perce reservation. Halting the battalion, Marcus rode to the crest of the low ridge with Simon Oliver and Lieutenant Brandt. Below, the waters of the Clearwater River sparkled.

"Have Captain Lemaster assume command of the battalion, John," Marcus directed. "You and I and Simon are going to pay Bright Sky a visit. Advise Cap-

21

tain Lemaster that if we are not back within three hours, he is to assume a hostile condition exists and act accordingly."

"Yes, sir!" The lieutenant saluted and rode off to relay his instructions to A Company's commanding officer. When he returned, the trio headed their mounts down the slope toward the village, which lay a short distance downstream just beyond the bend of the river.

They passed the legacy of the recent fight—five grave mounds, piled with rock that marked the last resting places of their fallen comrades. It was like Bright Sky to see to it that the soldiers had had a Christian burial. It was what Marcus admired about the man.

Rounding the river bend, Marcus abruptly signaled a halt. There was no village. All that remained was one lonely tipi, from which a thin wisp of smoke curled upward, hanging for a moment before dissipating in the haze of the late summer afternoon. Marcus glanced at Simon. The scout shrugged.

"Appears your Indians have high-tailed it, Marcus."

"It would seem so, my friend," Marcus said. "Let's take a look."

The three halted in front of the tipi. While Brandt remained on his horse, Marcus and Simon dismounted and cautiously entered.

As Marcus and Simon stepped into the dim interior, the light fron the flames of a small fire revealed the form of an aged Nez Perce man.

Their presence seemed not to disturb him. Eyes closed and hunched beneath an old blanket, he rocked gently back and forth, softly chanting the words to some ancient tribal elegy.

Marcus and Simon sat down. "Where is the village, old man?" Marcus asked. When there was no response, he repeated the question, this time more forcefully. "The village, where is it?"

Presently, the old man opened his eyes, looked at the two men seated across the fire from him, a toothless grin spreading across his leathery, wizened features.

"After buffalo. Gone after buffalo," he said, pointing a crooked, bony finger in no particular direction.

"Which way, old man?" Marcus asked.

"After buffalo," the man repeated.

Marcus looked at Simon and shook his head. Getting to their feet, the two men started out.

Stepping outside, Marcus and Simon walked towards Brandt.

"Too old to keep up so they left him," the scout observed.

"Never could get used to it," Marcus said.

Simon Oliver shrugged. "Their way."

They reached Brandt. "Advise Captain Lemaster that we will bivouac here," Marcus directed Lieutenant Brandt. "Oh, and, John, see that the old man is taken care of, will you?"

"Yes, sir," Brandt responded, and rode off.

"If you were the Nez Perce, where would you head, Simon?" Marcus asked, turning back to the scout.

Simon Oliver removed his battered, sweat-stained Stetson, passing a sun blackened hand across his brow.

"A fair question, Marcus," he answered at length. "Like the old man said, after buffalo. Won't be easy to support a band that size, especially with all them women and children."

Marcus nodded. "Shouldn't take much to follow a trail like that, Simon. You reckon you're equal to that challenge?" He grinned.

"I'll manage, Marcus."

"Watch your step, Simon. Bright Sky knows you'll be coming."

"You worried 'bout me, Marcus? I'm touched."

"Don't let it go to your head. If something happened to you, I'd be terribly inconvenienced."

Simon Oliver grinned, touched his hat and lifted the reins of his gelding. "Have your soldier boys get their butts ready. I've a feeling they kin figure to spend a lot of time in the saddle."

"Keep me posted, Simon."

Simon Oliver threw Marcus a casual salute, then wheeled his mount around in a sharp, near-foot spin. Quickly, he was gone.

Cavanaugh rode back to the battalion. He found Lieutenant Brandt. "Johnny, send a courier to the fort, advising Major Damon to be ready to move immediately, and notify department headquarters that the Nez Perce have left the reservation and that we will pursue at first light."

"Yes, sir," Brandt replied, and started off to select a courier.

In the gathering darkness, Marcus Cavanaugh contrasted the difference the past twenty-four hours had brought to his life. At this time yesterday he had been enjoying the pleasure of Elizabeth's company and tonight it looked as if he was on the threshold of an Indian war no one wanted.

Chapter Four

"They're movin' south, Marcus," Simon reported to Cavanaugh as Brandt handed the two others a tin of steaming hot coffee. It had taken him only ten hours to track the Indians and make his way back to the encampment. "No way to tell exactly where they're headed, but if it's after buffalo they've got to cross the mountains."

The scout paused to take a drink of coffee, shivering slightly in the chill morning air. "Orlo Pass gets my vote," he said continuing, " 'cause nothin' else makes much sense, given the size of that band. Means they'd move through Lobo Canyon on the other side."

Marcus nodded thoughtfully. "How many you figure?"

The scout pursed his lips. "Pretty good size band. Hard to say how many warriors. Couple of hundred, I 'spect."

"How long to Lobo?" Marcus asked. "Let's see that map, John."

The scout knelt down to study the map that Lieutenant Brandt unrolled and spread out on the ground. Simon frowned, pursing his lips. "For the Indians, three days."

"And for the troops from Fort Casey . . . ?"

Simon shrugged, tracing a line on the map with his forefinger. "Well, the distance is greater for them, but it shouldn't take near as long, Marcus. They could slip over North Pass, here, which is easy enough, then slide down along the east side of the mountains to Lobo. Two days tops, Marcus."

Marcus swirled the remaining coffee around in the bottom of his cup, pondering the plan that was forming in his mind. "Take a courier a day to get back to Casey," he said, thinking aloud. "That means we could have Major Damon waiting on the other side of Lobo Canyon in three days. And with us right behind the Indians, then it's just a matter of closing the pincers."

"But that's impossible," Brandt interrupted. "We're already a day behind the Indians. So it will take us four days to reach the canyon. And that's too late to block the Indians in."

The colonel glanced up, mentally scaling the thickly timbered slopes that rose up above them like towering gray sentinels in the dawn mist.

"You thinkin' what I think you're thinkin'?" Simon asked, watching Cavanaugh gaze at the hills.

Marcus grinned. "If we went over, rather than around those hills I bet we'd about gain that day we need, Simon."

"Be advised it's a tough haul, Marcus."

"You find us a way over and we'll manage, Simon." Cavanaugh turned to Lieutenant Brandt. "Send a courier to Fort Casey, John. Advise Major Damon to take up a blocking position at the mouth of Lobo Canyon.

Maybe seeing Damon ahead and knowing we're on their back trail will persuade Bright Sky to turn back."

"Frankly, sir, I doubt it," Brandt opined as he marched off.

"So do I," Marcus agreed, "but it's worth a try."

Brandt returned a moment later and behind him Marcus heard the thudding hooves of the departing courier's mount.

"Boots and saddles in thirty minutes, John," Marcus said, adding, "From here on, no bugle calls."

"Right, sir."

Less than a half-hour found the battalion climbing steadily upward, single file, through the forested slopes of the Wolf Mountains. The light ground fog to which they had awakened was slowly dissipating, giving way to the heat of the late summer sun. The steepness of the grade was such that Marcus ordered the column to dismount and walk fifteen minutes each hour.

Overhead, a cerulean sky deepened in intensity. The day grew warmer, and by mid-morning horses and riders were sweating profusely. At noon Marcus ordered a halt and permitted the men to build small coffee fires.

"We're right on schedule," he announced. "We ought to reach Lobo Canyon before dark the day after tomorrow."

Major Israel Damon sat at his desk, studying the dispatch handed him by the Colonel Cavanaugh's courier fifteen minutes earlier. The directive, written a day earlier, was clear enough. He was to march immediately with the remaining companies of the regiment and cut off the Nez Perce march at Lobo Canyon.

There was a sense of urgency about the order, both expressed and implied. What he found unsettling was the earlier communique from department headquarters. The communique directed that citizen volunteers throughout the region be used to quell the Nez Perce uprising and return the Indians to their reservation. More specifically, he was ordered to absorb one of these local groups, known as the Ramsey Rangers, into his command.

Word about the Nez Perce had swept among the settlers like wildfire, and the uprising had already begun to grow out of all proportion to its real nature. The local citizenry, fearing for life, limb and property, felt compelled to provide for the common defense by organizing companies of citizen soldiers. Now, apparently they had managed to exert enough political pressure to receive grudging recognition from the army, who like it or not, was forced to acknowledge their presence.

Israel Damon dropped the communique from department headquarters on the desk, arose and walked over to the window, his hands clasped behind his back, pondering the dilemma that had been thrust upon him.

The whole damn business was political and preposterous, but he had no choice but to wait for the rangers. And they wouldn't arrive until late the next day. That meant he wouldn't have enough time to reach Lobo Canyon when the colonel expected him there. He shook his head, with the certain feeling of being caught between a rock and hard place.

On the second day the soldiers continued the long arduous journey up Wolf Mountain. Marcus knew that sometime today Major Damon and his troops would arrive to block the mouth of Lobo Canyon. And by tomorrow he and his troops would arrive to block the rear trail at the Orlo Pass. So it was time to dispatch Simon to sneak around the Indians to find Major Damon.

"Instruct him to announce to Bright Sky tommorrow

that the Indians are trapped in the canyon," Marcus told Simon. "The chief will have no choice but to surrender." The scout left immediately.

Although Cavanaugh still felt that his pincer strategy was a good military plan, he had an uneasy feeling that something was not quite right. It was part of the warning mechanism honed to a fine degree by years of campaigning.

The Nez Perce band moved steadily if more slowly than Bright Sky would have preferred under the circumstances. But they could travel no faster than the slowest among them. If all went well, another two days would find them crossing Orlo Pass and moving down through Lobo Canyon along a time honored route, leading from their ancestral home to the great buffalo pastures that lay east of the mountains.

From atop his roan mare, Bright Sky watched the cavalcade file past, his entire people in transit, hauling all of their worldly possessions. There were old ones, with their shuffling gait, women with babies at their breasts, children of all ages.

He turned his mare and rode back through the procession, reflecting on their position, wondering if there was anything he had overlooked. Though the soldiers had not interfered with their journey so far, it was only a matter of time. His old friend, Marcus Cavanaugh, would not be turned back easily. Like himself, Marcus Cavanaugh would do what had to be done.

Little Raven had reported that the soldiers were indeed following. They could travel faster, and would eventually catch up. Raven had proposed a strategy that called for the warriors to travel behind the band and keep the pursuing soldiers at bay, allowing the others to continue unimpeded. Even now Raven's warriors were preparing a sortie against Marcus Cavanaugh's blue-coated soldiers.

On the third day Marcus watched the battalion move up the narrow trail beneath gathering cloud cover. The top of the mountain was only an hour or so away. In the distance thunder rumbled ominously and a steady breeze began to whistle over the crest of the ridge.

The thunder grew louder as they ascended the slope. On the far ridge a bolt of lightning flashed, followed by another. Presently droplets of rain began pelting the battalion, picking up in intensity, and slacking off.

Some three hours later, in what continued to be a blustery, showery afternoon, only about half the men were over the top, while the rest were still struggling up the slippery trail. Marcus could make out the figure of Simon Oliver moving toward him, his slicker flapping in the wind-driven rain that pounded them with a sudden intensity.

"Did you get through to Major Damon?" Marcus asked anxiously.

"He's not at Lobo Canyon." Simon replied grimly. "In fact, there no sign at all of him and his men."

Marcus looked stunned.

From his hiding place, Little Raven watched the column of soldiers work its way over the pass. He could almost hear the heavy, labored breathing of the big, grain-fed cavalry mounts. His warriors were well concealed, positioned behind brush, boulders and deadfalls.

Somewhere in the column of soldiers was a leader named Marcus Cavanaugh. His own memory of the soldier chief was vague. Privately, he found it difficult to appreciate his brother's deep feeling for this white soldier, but respecting Bright Sky as he did, Raven ac-

30

cepted his brother's sentiment. At the same time he vowed that it would not interfere with his own sense of duty.

He saw his moment when the soldiers were at the apogee of their climb and most vulnerable. Half were still climbing the final hundred yards, while the other half had begun the descent into Lobo Canyon. Raven's warriors opened fire with an initial volley that immediately emptied half a dozen saddles. A smile of satisfaction came to Raven's face. It pleased him to see the soldiers stung so sharply. It would show them what the Nez Perce could do!

Marcus should have anticipated that Bright Sky would not allow the soldiers to follow undisturbed. The old warning mechanism failed him.

The Nez Perce warriors caught the troopers on each flank with a suddenness that quickly had the battalion in disarray. Firing from concealed positions, the Indians had the battalion in a vulnerable situation.

Marcus cursed under his breath. Dismounting, he turned his mount over to an orderly and dashed forward to the center of action. Around him, troopers were reacting wildly, firing at nothing in particular. The screams of plunging, terrified horses mingled with the shouts and curses of the troopers. Non-coms moved among the men in an effort to restore order.

Cavanaugh motioned to Lieutenant Brandt to join him.

"Get word to Lemaster. Tell him to get a line of skirmishers out on both flanks. We've got to break this up quick."

"Right," Brandt said, quickly leaving.

Unholstering his Colt, Marcus took quick aim at a darting figure and fired, feeling the big revolver buck in his hand. His target dropped. Spotting another behind a large deadfall, he fired again and then a third time.

Around them the air was heavy with the smell of powder smoke and filled with the flat hammering reports of the cavalry Springfields. Here and there a Winchester or Colt rounded out the cacophony.

Marcus saw Simon Oliver take careful aim and fire. Since it was seldom that the scout missed, Marcus figured there was a better than even chance some Nez Perce warrior was a casualty.

A ragged line of skirmishers moved out along both flanks, non-coms trying to exercise steadiness and some measure of fire control discipline. With the soldiers taking cover behind rocks and trees, for another hour the exchange of fire was heated. Gradually, it began to taper off. Then, as quickly as it had begun, it was over.

The Nez Perce left as stealthily as they had hidden themselves. But they had not been driven off by the troops. They had merely accomplished what they set out to do.

As soon as some semblance of order had been restored and a perimeter defense set up, Marcus directed Johnny Brandt to tally up the casualties. In all, they had suffered five killed and fourteen wounded. Worst of all they had accomplished nothing. If the casualties had been the price of success it would not have been entirely in vain. But now Bright Sky had seized the initiative and worked it to his advantage.

"Where the hell was that support, Colonel?" Stephen Lemaster, the commander of B Company, asked.

Marcus looked at him steadily. "Obviously not here, Captain." Privately, he was asking the same question, though of course he could hardly afford to let that show.

Lemaster grunted, turned and walked back to his company.

Lemaster's personality often clashed with Marcus Cavanaugh's, but Lemaster was an able officer who could be depended on in a tight situation. A good commander, Marcus believed, took advantage of a subordinate's assets, while working around his weaknesses.

In any case, if Damon had been on hand as expected, they would now be herding Bright Sky's band back to the reservation. Instead, here he was with casualties and the Nez Perce still on the loose. The general would love this, he thought wryly. Damon's explanation had better be good. Having missed this opportunity to stop Bright Sky meant that now the job would be twice as tough.

Chapter Five

Despite the fatigue of a week's hard travel, the mood of the Nez Perce Indians had changed dramatically, fueled by the excitement of returning warriors, jubilant with the heady wine of their victory over the soldiers.

It warmed Bright Sky to see these young men sharing their exploits with admiring villagers. The stories related there today would be recounted to future generations, reminding them of the bravery of their ancestors.

Although Raven's warriors had won a victory over the soldiers and had a right to feel proud of their accomplishment, they had to guard against overconfidence. But the people would need the strength of such moments to carry them though the dark, difficult days ahead.

Later, Michael Bright Sky sat alone, facing the dwindling fire. The night chill deepened. One morning soon they would find ice on the water. That thought reminded him of the urgency of their flight.

The council had decided they would head for Canada, Land of the Grandmother, where Sitting Bull's Sioux now lived safe from the blue coats. Perhaps the Nez Perce could also find peace in that country. The distance was long and the way hard. Moreover, the country beyond the Firehole Valley was largely unknown to the Nez Perce.

As best he understood it, Bright Sky travelled the route in his mind. It was a two-day journey across the rugged Sweetwater Mountains to the valley of the Firehole River, a long-time camping place for Nez Perce hunting parties in search of buffalo. From the Firehole River, they would go on to the place of the great water spouts and stinking springs. There, they would turn toward the north, crossing the two great rivers the white people knew as Yellowstone and Missouri, until at last they reached mighty Horsetooth Mountain. He felt certain this sacred mountain of the Sioux would extend its hospitality to the Nez Perce as well. Beyond Horsetooth, it was only two sleeps to the Grandmother Land. But deep in his heart, Michael Bright Sky did not believe his people would be successful. They could hold back the blue coats only for so long. Eventually, he felt, the soldiers would prevail.

The soft sound of a moccasined foot came to him. He looked up to see Little Raven.

"I think we stung the blue coats today, my brother," he said, taking a seat across the fire.

Bright Sky nodded. "Yes and we shall pay for it, too."

Little Raven scoffed. "You worry too much. Like an old woman."

"This thing we do is madness, brother. We cannot possibly hope to outrun the soldiers. We may sting them a little, but in the end they will overwhelm us."

"Aaah!" Little Raven growled and stood up. "What we did today we can do tomorrow!"

35

"And the day after that?" Bright Sky asked.

"We must deal with one day at a time, brother," Little Raven answered, gesturing with a clenched fist for emphasis.

"And what of the women and children? What of the old ones?" Bright Sky asked softly. "Feel the air. It grows cold. The people will need more than stories to fill their bellies and keep them warm."

"Freedom is not cheap," Little Raven retorted, anger rising in his voice. "Our people are strong. They will survive."

"Spoken like a warrior," Bright Sky said. He walked over and placed his hand on his brother's shoulder. "And that is why you are a warrior. But I must concern myself with all of our people. And I must have your help, brother. If we are to reach the Grandmother Country it will take all of our skill and courage, not just as warriors but as a people."

He looked steadily into the eyes of Little Raven, who shifted uncomfortably. It had always been like this, for as long as he could remember. Bright Sky and those words of his . . . and those eyes. How could one refuse him?

Little Raven nodded. "I wish to do all I can. Did you think otherwise?"

Bright Sky shook his head. "No. I knew I could rely on you." He turned and walked back to resume his seat in front of the fire, adding a small piece of wood, staring thoughtfully as the flames bit into the fresh fuel.

"Marcus Cavanaugh will not give up easily," he said. "I know him. You hurt them yesterday, that is true. But beware, brother. He is not a man to be trifled with, nor will it be easy to surprise him again."

"Wise brother, I think you have a plan," Little Raven said.

Bright Sky nodded, permitting himself the luxury of a brief smile. "I do have an idea. You will take all but a few warriors, circle around behind the soldiers and attack them while they are crossing the Sweetwater Pass. They will not expect an attack from the rear."

With a stick he quickly traced a few lines in the dirt, illustrating his strategy.

Little Raven frowned. "A dangerous plan, brother."

"True, the risk is great, but consider this. We need time for our people to get safely beyond the reach of the soldiers," Bright Sky pointed out. "You and your warriors can gain that time for us."

Little Raven nodded. "You are right as usual. Maybe you should have been a warrior."

"Each man is a warrior in his own way," Bright Sky said. "We shall see how well Marcus Cavanaugh fares against real warriors, eh, brother?"

Little Raven flashed a broad grin. "Talk like that makes my heart soar."

"I thought it would," Bright Sky said. "Ride carefully, my brother."

"And you, brother. Be no less careful." Little Raven turned and left, leaving Bright Sky alone to feel the chill of his own judgment.

Major Israel Damon was in trouble, but there was little he could do about it. As a result of having to wait for the volunteers, who arrived mostly hungover, he was going to be late reaching Lobo Canyon, and the colonel was not going to be pleased.

To make matters worse, a second communique had arrived from General Abrams just before he left, exhorting Colonel Cavanaugh to corral these Indians and get them back on the reservation before the uprising turned into a major incident.

The major now rode at the head of a column that numbered nearly five hundred, including eighty-four civilian soldiers, for whom he had nothing but total disdain. They called themselves the Ramsey Rifles. The name stuck in his craw. Their arrogance was nauseating, not to mention their habits.

A Civil War veteran, Damon had to admit that without the volunteers there would never have been a victory parade down Pennsylvania Avenue. But those volunteers were soldiers, at least after a while they were. This bunch, on the other hand, was a mob with little in the way of organization and no discipline. It would have to be watched closely.

Israel Damon stood as a classic example of an officer whose career had been effectively ended by one mistake. Ten years earlier, Damon, then a young major, launched a successful dawn attack against what turned out to be a friendly Indian village. The band of hostiles he sought was encamped a few miles away.

Unfortunately for Damon, the government had been in the process of implementing a new peace policy toward the tribes, and he was held up as an example of an overly aggressive militarist. He hadn't really violated any orders, however, so they couldn't court-martial him, but he was made an object lesson. His career was stone-walled from that time forward. Israel Damon would retire a major regardless of what he did during the rest of his time in the army.

There were so many moments when the dim prospect of his future resulted in a depression which found him seeking solace in a bottle that his wife of fifteen years had finally left him. Once considered one of the army's promising young officers, Damon had gotten his majority early and his star was in its ascendancy. But a man's fortunes could shift quickly.

Not infrequently he imagined himself in one vital confrontation wherein the record of Israel Damon would be set straight and the stigma of the past would be erased forever. How often had he sworn to himself that should the opportunity present itself he would not let it pass. The present situation, however, seemed a continuation of his misfortune. Once again, he would pay the price for circumstances not of his making.

His thoughts were interrupted by the voice of a young second lieutenant. "Excuse me, sir. Did you plan on a noon halt?"

"Aaah, yes, Lieutenant," he said, a bit embarrassed at his oversight. "We'll stop for an hour. The men may build coffee fires. See that pickets are posted."

"Yes, sir." The lieutenant saluted with a crispness reserved exclusively for officers of his rank and station.

As had become his custom, Israel Damon sipped the coffee prepared by his orderly alone. The senior officers of the regiment avoided him. It was not out of any real personal dislike of the man, but, sensing a troubled man who preferred his own company, they chose not to intrude. There was also Israel's reputation and an irrational fear that the stigma associated with it might attach itself to others.In his own way Israel Damon understood this and accepted it as part of the cross he bore.

The sky above was darkening with thunderstorms as the regiment resumed its journey. Barring any unforeseen difficulties they ought to reach Lobo Canyon by sunset.

Anson Demarest, a portly, red-bearded individual who had more or less been elected captain of the citizen volunteers, galloped up alongside Israel, hauling his mount to a walk once he was abreast of the major. The man's breath stunk of whiskey and his eyes were red-rimmed.

"Drink, Major?" he asked, offering Damon a flask.

Damon looked at him coldly. "No. And just for the record, I don't want to see that flask again. I'll arrest any man I catch drinking, including you Demarest."

Anson Demarest took another swig from the flask and wiped his grizzled features with the back of a dirty coat sleeve. "Strange talk comin' from a man as partial to the bottle as you, Major," he said with a sardonic curl to his upper lip.

Israel Damon glared at the man and suppressed the urge to strike him. "Get out of here, Demarest, and stay out of my way."

Anson Demarest was a boor and at the moment slightly drunk. He was not, however, stupid. He had no trouble recognizing the flat, ugly threat behind the major's words. He reined his mount around and galloped back to his men.

The thunder that had been building as they rode rumbled closer. Rain began to splatter down, first in large droplets, then tightening to a fine bead with increasing intensity. Once the sensation of being drenched had passed, Israel Damon found that the drumming of the rain against his body had a certain soothing effect that was almost welcome.

Marcus Cavanaugh read the two directives from General Abrams that Israel Damon had handed him upon his arrival thirty minutes earlier. Damon sat on a nearby stump, working on his second cup of coffee.

Marcus was angry. "Damn! What does the general think we're doing out here?" he demanded from no one in particular. "Headquarters seems to regard this as a cattle roundup." He started to crumple the messages, then thought better of it.

"Here, John, better file these," he said, handing the papers to Lieutenant Brandt.

He poured himself a cup of coffee, and addressed Major Damon in the process. "I needed you yesterday, Major."

"I wanted to be here, sir," Damon replied simply.

Marcus nodded. "You had a direct order from me."

"Yes, sir, but in view of the directive from headquarters, I felt I had no choice but to wait."

Marcus looked at him for a long moment. "Major, you know as well as I do that a commander on the spot has the right to interpret an order according to circumstances that confront him. That's what command is all about, Major. The order from headquarters was issued without knowledge of my situation. You had that knowledge. You knew I was counting on your support."

Israel Damon got to his feet and tossed the remains of his coffee into the fire. "I'm sorry, Colonel, but the decision was mine to make."

"And you made it with your career in mind, Major!" Marcus put in, regretting the statement even as he uttered it.

Israel Damon flushed and stammered. "I resent that accusation, Colonel . . . "

Marcus waved him off. "That will be all for now, Major. I want this thing put behind us. We've got a job to do, and it may well take every man in this regiment, including yourself. Is that clear?"

Damon nodded.

"Get some rest, Major."

Marcus watched him stride off. A good officer ruined by a bad system? No, Israel Damon, was simply a man who succumbed to himself, a condition that was open to change whenever the man so desired it. Maybe this campaign would be the crucible of change for Israel Damon. Marcus hoped so.

Chapter Six

Once again the battalion was threading its way up a steep timbered hillside, wending its way toward the summit. Above, a sky of pale washed blue had replaced the gunmetal gray canopy of yesterday's storm. Around them, the foliage dripped with moisture and steam rose from the breaths of man and horse alike as the column struggled upward. The soldiers were already perspiring despite the bone chilling dampness of the early morning.

"We'll halt for half an hour this side of the summit, Lieutenant," Cavanaugh ordered. "But no fires. The men will have to be satisfied with a cold breakfast."

John Brandt nodded. "Bright Sky can't be that far ahead, Colonel. They had to cross Sweetwater Pass same as we're doing and it ought to have been tougher on them than us."

"That's my guess, too," Marcus agreed. "We should know more when Simon gets back."

Half an hour later, Simon Oliver reined his mount

42

up alongside Marcus, his face haggard from being almost constantly in the saddle the past five days.

"Well, I didn't see 'em, but they're headin' east, Marcus. My guess is they'll push hard for the Firehole River and hole up there for a day or two. They've got enough of a jump on us to make it work. Good spot to take a breather. Plenty of grass and there's apt to be buffalo around."

Marcus nodded. "Makes sense. And that means we've got to stay after them, Simon. We've got a chance to close that gap."

The scout nodded wearily.

"In the meantime, you better get a little sleep," Marcus said, flashing a grin.

"You don't strike me as quite pretty enough to be a nurse, though I'm glad to see you ain't lost your sense of humor, Marcus."

Bright sun and a canopy of clear blue greeted the battalion as it finally topped the crest of Sweetwater Pass. The view was stunning. Behind them and to the north rose high granite spires, dusted with snow from yesterday's storm. Ahead, the continuous ocean of pine and spruce flowed down to the valley floor below.

It was a breathtaking vista, Marcus had to admit, and it seemed a shame to intrude on the serenity. But regardless of how much he hoped it turned out otherwise, Marcus knew full well his presence was likely to result in violence.

The Nez Perce warriors worked their way slowly and skillfully toward the crest of the divide. It had been a long, difficult approach, necessitating considerable caution to avoid detection. Nearing the summit, the warriors had dismounted, and after muzzling their horses, resumed the climb on foot, pulling the horses behind them.

Little Raven took in the entire perimeter of his advance with a sweeping, practiced glance that left him satisfied with the way his tactic was evolving. Next to him, Stone Bear was breathing heavily and sweating profusely. When Stone Bear struggled, one knew it had indeed been a hard climb. He was a fine warrior, not terribly imaginative, but strong and dependable as the fine spotted horses for which the Nez Perce were well known.

Fifty yards below the crest, they halted, allowing time for men and animals to fill their aching lungs with the thin, fresh air.

"Are you ready to sting the soldiers again, Bear?" Raven asked, flashing a smile.

Stone Bear nodded. "This time it will be even better."

"And so it will," Raven agreed. Swinging easily aboard his mount he kneed him forward, and was followed by the others. Just this side of the crest, they paused one final time. According to a scout, the soldiers were just ahead and expecting nothing from behind.

A smile of satisfaction crossed Raven's face. Raising his right arm, his hand clenched around the Winchester, he gestured once. Then he spurred his horse over the crest with a fierce scream and drove down on the trailing elements of the Eleventh Cavalry, followed closely by his brother warriors.

The battalion had completed its brief halt and was in the process of resuming its forward movement when a fusillade of shots shattered the pristine silence of the late morning. The one thing Cavanaugh and his officers had not expected was an attack from the rear.

"Lemaster's formed a line behind us," Brandt reported, riding up quickly beside the colonel. "But he says to send help fast."

The volume of fire swelled, the flat boom of the army Springfields mingling with reports from the assorted Indian weapons.

"John, find Simon. Tell him to get his tail over here fast. Then tell Marchant to get back here with A Company."

Brandt nodded and left to carry out his instructions. Glancing around, Marcus watched Lemaster dispersing his command to meet the threat. He moved over to where his senior company commander was issuing orders.

The Nez Perce had driven into the tail end of the column like a thunderclap, after which they had dismounted. In keeping with their usual skilled tactics, they pursued the attack from cover behind trees and deadfalls.

Frustrated by an absence of visible targets, the troopers were firing wildly despite the efforts of Lemaster and his non-commissioned officers to maintain fire control discipline.

Marcus moved up alongside Lemaster just as an orderly next to B Company's commanding officer pitched forward, blood spurting from the bullet hole in his neck.

"We're outnumbered, Colonel," Lemaster shouted over the roar of rifle fire. "I've got everyone committed."

"A Company's on the way," Marcus said, studying the perimeter of action. It appeared Lemaster was right. What's more, the Nez Perce seemed to be drawing the perimeter tighter.

Simon Oliver moved in beside him. Ejecting a thin

stream of tobacco off to the side, he casually raised a fifty caliber Sharps to his shoulder, aimed and fired. The boom of the weapon overpowered the reports of the cavalry Springfields.

"We got caught with our drawers down around our ankles, Simon."

"I allow we did at that, Marcus," he agreed, squeezing off another shot.

When it arrived, the lead platoon of A Company was a welcome sight. Marcus directed it to reinforce the left flank where the pressure seemed greatest. The remainder of Marchant's company was not far behind. Like the first platoon they were promptly rushed into the fray, adding the weight of their Springfields to those of B Company.

With the extra support, Marcus launched a counterattack and gradually regained the initiative. By early afternoon the Nez Perce had withdrawn. Once again they had accomplished their mission. For the moment, the fox had bested the hounds.

The next morning, there had been ice to skim off the tops of the water buckets. The day gave promise of being a good one, but the signs of summer preparing to give way to fall grew increasingly evident with each passing day.

Breakfast fires burned throughout the area as the men boiled water for coffee and sought the companionship of the flames against the morning chill.

Sipping his own coffee, Marcus looked over his command. Across the way, hospital orderlies and an assistant surgeon were preparing the wounded for evacuation. Elsewhere, company commanders and first sergeants were readying their men for what promised to be a day of vigorous pursuit.

46

Marcus had always appreciated this time of the day, the first stirrings of a command in the early morning, the smell of freshly brewed coffee, the earthy sights and sounds of a disciplined body of men preparing themselves for a day's campaigning. For two decades army life had given him a sense of belonging that was never more evident than at moments such as this.

As a result of Israel Damon's arrival, his force now included eight of the regiment's full complement of twelve companies, something in excess of six hundred men. He found himself hoping that they'd be able to bring this affair to a quick and merciful conclusion. There was no question in his mind as to the ultimate outcome. What troubled him was the price both sides could wind up paying before that end was achieved, especially now that politics were beginning to complicate matters.

He reached into the breast pocket of his blouse and took out the second dispatch from department headquarters, brought in late yesterday by a tired courier on a lathered mount. The message reflected the pressure that Abrams was feeling from Washington and passing on to Marcus Cavanaugh. That was the way the system worked, although that did little to assuage the anger and frustration Marcus experienced as commander on the spot.

He reread the dispatch wanting to make certain he understood the spirit as well as the word.

To Col. M. Cavanaugh, Cmd'g 11th Cavalry:
Colonel:You are directed to maintain pursuit of the Nez Perce; recover and return them to their agency without delay. You are advised to use discretion in carrying out these orders, as situation sensitive and it is desirable to achieve objective

with minimum cost. I will join you with reinforcements as quickly as circumstances permit.
Brig. Gen. C. Abrams, Commanding Dept

Marcus shook his head slowly. "Does he think I'm
dragging my feet? Just how am I to bring all of this
about?"

Simon Oliver sliced a strip of tobacco from a half-
used plug, using the flat of his blade to put the sub-
stance in his mouth. "Well, I allow you could issue 'em
a invitation, Marcus," he suggested dryly.

"I'm touched by your sensitivity to my problem,
Simon," Marcus snorted.

"Jest tryin' to help, Colonel."

"Well, who knows, we might have more luck that
way." He turned to his adjutant. "Lieutenant Brandt,
officers' call in fifteen minutes."

When the officers had gathered Marcus brought
them up to date on the directive from headquarters and
spelled out their strategy, which in essence would be
to press forward as quickly as possible. They were in
a position to move faster than the Nez Perce and it was
his intention to take advantage of that fact. Their best
bet, Marcus felt, was to locate and surprise the tribe in
a dawn attack.

"Begging your pardon, Colonel, but that would
seem to conflict with departmental orders," Major
Damon pointed out.

"I'm aware of that possibility, Major, and that's a responsibility I'll have to assume."

"Of course, sir."

Marcus had mixed feelings about his second-in-
command. On the one hand he recognized the man's
potential, suppressed now by one mistake. Marcus appreciated what such a mistake could do to a man's ca-

reer, but he also believed an individual had the power to rise above a mistake or remain its prisoner. Israel Damon, he felt, had chosen the latter.

What concerned Marcus at the moment was to what extent the major's past might influence his behavior in the here and now. Could he be depended on? Marcus wasn't sure. He did feel that Damon deserved a chance and to the extent it didn't jeopardize the command, Marcus intended to see he got it.

"I'm dividing the regiment," Marcus said. A, B, C and D Companies will comprise the first battalion under Captain Lemaster. I will accompany. Major Damon will command E, F, G and H. For the moment all eight companies will travel together. Boots and saddles in thirty minutes. Any questions, gentlemen?"

"What about us volunteers, Colonel?"

Marcus looked at the scrubby, pork-jowled features of Anson Demarest. "What about them, Mr. Demarest?"

"Well, you ain't said where we fit in this plan."

"That's right," Marcus said. "I want to make sure I use your volunteers in the best possible way, Mr. Demarest."

Anson Demarest cleared his throat and spat off to the side, thoroughly confused. He sensed somehow he was being had, but didn't quite know how to respond. He felt his face coloring. Across the way, Marcus saw Simon Oliver rolling his eyes heavenward.

"For the time being, Mr. Demarest, the volunteers will remain with Major Damon's battalion." He noted Israel Damon stiffening as the announcement was made.

"Very well, gentlemen. You may see to your commands. Lieutenant Brandt will issue the order of march."

As the company commanders headed back to their respective commands, Simon Oliver walked over to Marcus, his pale green eyes hosting a glint of amusement.

"I'd hope you figure to be least as considerate of your scouts as them volunteers, Colonel."

"At least, Simon, at least."

"I'm mighty relieved," the scout admitted, flashing a wry grin beneath the sweeping, tawny mustache. "For a time there, you had me worried, Marcus."

Marcus looked at his chief scout. "Where's our best chance of catching them at a disadvantage, Simon?" Unrolling the worn map of the area, he studied it carefully.

Simon Oliver pulled thoughtfully on the end of his mustache, pondering the question.

"I'm still thinkin' they're headin' for the Firehole, and that's where I'd figure to drop in and say howdy, was I you."

"They could turn north, Simon. Could be buffalo in that direction, too."

The scout shook his head. "Don't think so, Marcus. They know that Firehole country. It's special to them. That's where I'd head if I was Bright Sky, which of course I ain't, you understand."

"Perfectly," Marcus said. "Maybe you should have been an Indian, Simon."

"Maybe I am, Marcus, maybe I am."

Chapter Seven

Bright Sky watched his people as they attended to their daily chores. Despite the hardships of the past several days, he sensed a bright new spirit in their demeanor and it pleased him to see them this way.

A group of small boys ran toward him, pursuing an old ball, probably obtained from one of the many missionaries that had touched their lives in the past. Their yells and laughter filled him with a sense of satisfaction he had not tasted in recent times and he savored that feeling.

Perhaps his fears really were those of an old man, as Little Raven teased. The warriors had stung Marcus Cavanaugh a second time and shown the soldiers what would happen if the Nez Perce were pushed too hard. Yet there was a nagging sense of uneasiness that lurked within him. He scolded himself, scoffing at his fears. Little Raven's warriors would provide plenty of warning.

He walked slowly through the camp, nodding to some, speaking casually to others. This was the perfect spot to rest and gain strength for the remainder of their journey, which promised to be long and hard, especially when the snows came.

The sun overhead was a bright golden disk, flooding the valley with its warmth. Nearby, the sparkling waters of the Firehole River, from which the valley drew its name, flowed past the camp, its rippling movement a symphony of peace and harmony.

A small herd of buffalo had been located in the rich pasture lands just beyond the valley and the warriors had made several kills. The women were curing and preparing the meat for the lean times that were sure to follow this hour of plenty. A small portion of the buffalo harvest had been set aside for a feast that night. There would even be some dancing. Not like the old days, admittedly, but in a way perhaps even more meaningful because of what the people had been through.

He walked on through the camp and at the far end, he climbed a small rise to a secluded niche that overlooked the village. There, he drew into himself to ponder their future movements.

A fear gnawed at the very core of his being, a fear of being unequal to his great responsibility. He dared not express this to anyone, not even Swan, for to do so might infect the whole camp. It was a burden he must bear alone. He suspected Swan sensed something of what tore at her husband, for on occasion he caught her watching him with grave concern. At such moments he deeply regretted bringing such trouble into her life.

Here in the partially shadowed seclusion of this small sanctuary, Bright Sky sat with his back against a great boulder. A shaft of sunlight penetrated the arms of the surrounding firs, warming and soothing his troubled spirit. The sound of voices below awoke him. The sun had moved just enough to drain his sanctuary of light.

He roused himself and headed back to the village, where a hunting party had returned with another kill, this time a fat buffalo cow.

"Our meat supply grows, my brother," Little Raven shouted from atop his prancing Appaloosa, as Bright Sky approached.

Bright Sky smiled. "Yes, and we shall need it."

Little Raven swung down from his mount to walk alongside his brother. His strong, chiseled features made Bright Sky think of their grandfather, Elk Tooth, of whom Little Raven had no real memory. Many young women in the village would consider Little Raven a prize catch, but the latter had so far refused to acknowledge anyone in particular. Bright Sky smiled as he thought, remembering his own young manhood.

"Aaah, it is good to see you smile, brother," Little Raven said, breaking the silence.

"My thoughts were of easier matters than what we now face, little brother."

"We have done well," Little Raven declared, the pride evident in his voice. "And tonight our people will celebrate."

"Yes," Bright Sky agreed. "Tonight there will be much joy among the people. But let us not forget that our journey is far from over. It remains a long distance to the Grandmother Land, with winter ahead of us."

"And the long knives behind us," Little Raven added.

"Yes, brother, so let us celebrate but not so much so that we forget what faces us."

Little Raven laughed and the sound of his laughter was a tonic. "Rest easy, brother. There will be no surprises."

That evening around the pulsing light of the fires it seemed that Little Raven's assurance was well founded.

As the dancers swayed to the steady thump of drums, the people feasted on roast buffalo. Later, when the drums were stilled and the dancers slept with exhaustion, Bright Sky lay under the robe in his lodge, staring at the small firehole at the top. He felt good about the evening's festivities, but still harbored a nagging worry about his people's predicament. Next to him, Swan moved closer, sensing his concern. She said nothing, but let the closeness of her body remind him that she was there. The sleep that came to both of them was deep but troubled.

From his crouched position Simon Oliver peered through the darkness at the Nez Perce camp. The night chill was damp and penetrating, and his right leg tingled from a lack of circulation. Accordingly, the sound of drums and the distant glow of the firelight looked downright inviting. From somewhere in the village, a dog yapped, followed by a second one. And as he strained, listening, he could detect the horse herd.

He was certain there must be guards out, but in the hour spent in the cold chill, he hadn't seen nor heard a sign. Perhaps the Nez Perce somehow felt comfortable enough to celebrate without guards watching their back trail. In any case, it might be the edge the colonel was looking for. Rising stiffly to an erect position, he gave his legs a moment to regain full circulation then moved cautiously back to his tethered horse, two hundred yards away.

It was too dark to see his watch, but he guessed the time at ten or so. It had taken him two hours to locate the village, and he'd been there for an hour, more or less, which meant he would not get back to Marcus much before one a.m. However, that ought to give the regiment time enough to get there for a dawn attack.

Given the fact that the Nez Perce seemed in a celebrating mood, the timing would be perfect. Reaching his horse, he climbed into the saddle and headed back.

Cavanaugh's orderly, Corporal Theobald Ames, gently shook Marcus awake at one-thirty in the morning, informing him that Simon had returned from his mission. Struggling out of his blankets in the damp chill suggested, as it usually did, the advisability of another career. He stomped around, slapping his sides, thinking how good a cup of coffee would taste.

Simon Oliver approached.

"You might have been more considerate of a man's rest," Marcus muttered.

Simon shrugged. "Well, look at it this-a-way, Marcus. Bein' up and around you'll stay warmer."

"Some consolation," Marcus said. "What did you find?"

"Like I figured, they're camped along the Firehole, half a dozen miles from here. They're celebratin', Marcus. No sentries that I could see."

"I can't believe that, Simon."

"Seems strange to me as well, Marcus. My guess is that they figure you're far enough behind they can afford to take a breather. Nothin' else makes any sense."

Marcus nodded. "Well, let's not look a gift horse in the mouth. Ames!" he called out, "Roust out Lieutenant Brandt."

It was nearing three a.m. when the regiment stood to horse beneath a velvet, spangled sky. No fires were permitted and all had been cautioned against any unnecessary noise. Non-coms moved back and forth through their companies seeing to the readiness of their cold, grumpy charges.

"We'll make final troop dispositions later, Lieutenant Brandt," Marcus advised. "Get them started. Major Damon's wing can lead off."

"Very good, sir." Brandt moved off through the darkness to set the soldiers in motion.

As the column wound slowly through the blackness, the riders were barely able to discern the shape of the man and animal in front of them. The sounds of a large body of horsemen on the march emerged from all along the column, the squeak of saddle leather and the jingling of curb chains, horses snorting and breaking wind.

As he rode, Marcus found his thoughts suddenly on Elizabeth. She hadn't really been on his mind much the past few days—little other than the Nez Perce had been. Now, as he recalled their last night together, he found that the memory warmed him. His thoughts were interrupted by Simon Oliver coming up on his right.

"There's a decent size swale about a mile from the village, Marcus. Make a good spot to pass out your final orders."

"Lieutenant Brandt, advise Major Damon we'll muster about a mile and half from the village. Make sure he and his troops don't get lost, will you, Simon."

Marcus imagined a grin on the angular scout's features as he headed for the point of the column. The stygian blackness that had engulfed the soldiers when they set out two hours earlier was weakening in intensity as the night progressed toward dawn.

Within an hour the regiment had reached the assembly area. A light ground fog rose to cover the lower portions of men and animals, giving the command a ghostly appearance. Cavanaugh's company commanders moved up to join him.

"The village runs along the north side of the river,"

56

Marcus explained when they'd all gathered around. "My intention is to come at them from both ends."

Marcus glanced around the circle of faces before continuing. "Major Damon, your battalion will strike from the east end, pushing the village back against Captain Lemaster's battalion that will be advancing from the west. Between the two I think the village can be caught and contained. The pony herd is on the east end, so your battalion will also have the responsibility of isolating it from any Nez Perce who try to escape. I want that herd cut off. The sound of your guns will be the key for Captain Lemaster to move in."

"It will be difficult to coordinate such a maneuver, Colonel," Israel Damon pointed out.

Marcus nodded. "I recognize that, Major, but it's the best way to insure that the village doesn't break up and scatter." His eyes met those of Damon's. For a moment Marcus thought he detected fear, but he couldn't be sure. In any case there wasn't time to pursue the matter. He'd have to chance it.

"Simon figures you will need an hour to an hour and a half to move into position. It's nearly five now, so Lemaster will begin his attack at half-past six. That should give you plenty of time, Major. Simon will accompany you. Questions, gentlemen?"

Marcus glanced around, but if there were questions or comments none were voiced. "Very well, then. I'd like to remind you all that our objective is to return the Nez Perce to the agency. We are not here to see how much destruction we can wreak."

Out of the corner of his eye, Marcus saw Israel Damon wince. Immediately he regretted the last part of his statement.

"Let's try and make it as quick and clean as possible. I will remain with Captain Lemaster's battalion should you need to contact me. That's all. Good luck, gentlemen."

As the group disbanded, Marcus called to Israel Damon. "Oh, Major would you remain for a moment?"

Israel Damon hunched slightly in the damp chill, expecting the worst.

"I'm sorry, Major. I did not mean to suggest that . . . "

"I understand, Colonel. No offense taken."

It was the inflection in his voice more than the words that annoyed Marcus. "Look, Major. I don't have a lot of time to spend on this, so I'll be blunt. What a man does with his life is his business. When it affects this regiment it becomes my business. Understood?"

Israel Damon looked at him for a long moment. There was no sign of hostility, Marcus noted, but rather what almost seemed a sadness, and he found that strangely disquieting. Marcus wished he'd seen anger instead. As he watched Major Israel Damon walk away, he had the uncomfortable feeling that too much hinged on the performance of this man. And yet Damon's rank and station in the regiment made it virtually impossible to ignore the man.

Marcus walked through the early gray light of dawn to where Lieutenant Brandt and Captain Lemaster were ironing out final details. He found himself wishing that Damon was more like Lemaster, even though the latter was a hot head and tough to control at times. On the other hand, Damon also deserved a chance to redeem himself, and Marcus could only hope the price wouldn't prove too steep.

The companies moved into attack order. From downstream one of the village curs commenced barking, having detected something that disturbed him. Marcus

58

could only hope his canine sensitivity was not reacting to their presence. He lifted a slightly tarnished watch from his vest pocket and noted the time. It was almost five-thirty. Damon ought to be close. Glancing at the sky he saw the day's light had gradually taken hold. Across the lip of horizon a faint salmon-pink tint began to color the east.

He remembered the watch well. A West Point graduation present, it had remained with him throughout his career. The watch served as a reminder of the end of one way of life and the beginning of another. Like its owner, the watch was now a seasoned veteran, bearing the scars of many campaigns. He snapped it shut and put it away.

Presently, Johnny Brandt approached. "We're about as ready as we'll ever be, Colonel. It's nearly half-past five. Things are beginning to stir in the village."

Marcus nodded. "We wait, Lieutenant. Until we hear the sound of Damon's guns."

"Very good, sir."

From the Nez Perce village a second dog joined the first, adding to the cacophony. Dawn spread across the east, flooding the eastern horizon with a stunning beauty.

"We wait much longer we can forget about any surprise, Colonel," Lemaster muttered impatiently. Even as he was speaking the first flat reports of Damon's carbines floated down the valley toward them.

Captain Stephen Lemaster gave a signal and his battalion swung out of the swale and toward the Nez Perce camp, the sound of the shod hooves of four companies thundering through the fog enshrouded dawn.

Chapter Eight

Major Israel Damon wanted a drink, but stifled the urge to reach for the flask in his saddle bag. Next to him, Simon Oliver rode loose and relaxed. Damon envied the man. In point of fact he envied many men, sometimes without even being sure exactly why. One thing he was sure of though was that nobody envied Israel Damon. Not unless he were a fool.

In the budding light of the daybreak he could make out the Nez Perce village through the break in the trees ahead. Smoke curled from the tops of tipis. Near the center of the encampment, a figure emerged from one tipi and walked toward the river, while closer to this end, a pair of camp curs fought over the remains of something left from last night's feasting. Save for a few personal mounts, the main pony herd was on a beach just across the river. There was little doubt that the cavalry would have the element of surprise.

Calling his four company commanders together, the

major assigned responsibility for the pony herd to E Company, while F, G and H attacked the village itself.

"I'm startin' to get real upset about you reglar soldiers hoardin' all the fun and games," Anson Demarest growled.

Israel Damon looked at the man and decided there were few individuals he liked less than Demarest, the leader of the civilian volunteers.

"To begin with this is not a contest of fun and games. I repeat my order for your benefit. Your men will provide support, Mr. Demarest."

"Support, my ass, Major. I'll be damned if . . . "

"You either comply with my orders or I'll have you arrested and returned to Fort Casey under guard. Is that clear?"

Damon surprised himself with his own forcefulness. Demarest sensed he had pushed as hard as he dared and backed down, grumbling under his breath, "You ain't heard the last of this, Major."

As E company moved out and the others formed up for the attack, Damon felt his face perspire despite the damp chill in the dawn air. He was grateful for the low light and hoped his condition wasn't noticeable.

"Unless you want me off roundin' up them ponies, I'll ride along with you, Major," Simon Oliver offered.

"What? Oh, yes. Good idea, Mr. Oliver."

They were off with F and G Companies abreast, and H following as a reserve. A single shot from the carbine of F Company's adjutant got the ball rolling. Israel Damon rode at the front with Simon Oliver as the battalion advanced toward the village, the companies moving first at a trot, then breaking into a gallop.

The soldiers were two hundred yards out when the village awoke to their presence. Warriors stumbled from their lodges, a few with firearms, others with bows and a few arrows. Reacting quickly, they tried to disrupt the attack with carefully placed shots, but they were too few in number to turn back the soldiers.

In his tipi, Bright Sky came awake instantly at the sound of gunfire. Fear clutched at his insides. Next to him, Swan, too, had heard and recognized the dreaded sound.

"It is my fault. I should have known Marcus would be close at hand," he said stumbling to the lodge entrance.

Outside, his worst fears were instantly realized. The village was in total turmoil. Soldiers were attacking from two directions. Pockets of resistance were developing as warriors rallied to defend the tribe.

"You must help get the children and old ones to safety," Michael Bright Sky told Swan. 'Take them up there in the hills." He pointed to the sloping hillsides above the campsite, pockmarked with huge deadfalls and giant boulders.

"Please be careful," she urged him. Swan turned and was gone.

Quickly surveying the situation, Bright Sky spotted Little Raven and ran toward him. Around them the sound of firing intensified. He was conscious of casualties, powder smoke and chaos everywhere.

"It seems the soldiers have a sting of their own, my brother," Bright Sky said grimly as he approached.

Israel Damon heard firing off to his left rear and knew that E Company was busy with the pony herd. To his immediate front he became aware of an increasing number of non-combatants spilling out of the tipis and lodges, old women and young mothers with small children and babies. Resistance was mounting, too, as more warriors began to move in and make their presence felt.

From the far end of the village the sound of firing meant that Cavanaugh was moving in with Lemaster's battalion. Damon's own troopers were firing now, the boom of their 45-70 Springfields a rising crescendo of sound that ruptured the early morning stillness.

With Army Colt in hand, Major Israel Damon was at the front of his surging battalion when a woman and child burst from a tipi just ahead of him and to the right. For an instant he thought she was a warrior. He fired and saw her drop, then saw the child. In a flash, his own dark past returned with horror. He raised his arm abruptly, brought his battalion to a screeching halt, and ordered his companies to dismount and form a skirmish line. History would not repeat itself, and Major Israel Damon was determined not make the same mistake a second time.

Stunned by his order, it took Damon's battalion a moment to understand that he was calling off the attack and assuming the defensive.

"Major, what in hell goes?" Simon Oliver shouted, his voice filled with incredulity.

"If you can't see what's happening here, Mr. Oliver, I've no time to explain." Damon turned away to seek out his aide, leaving in his wake a stunned and puzzled chief of scouts.

His line pulled back from its advance to a position that offered limited cover. The shallow river was at the battalions back. Across the river horse holders guarded the battalion's mounts.

The battalion had already suffered perhaps a dozen casualties. Glancing up and down the line he noted two more casualties. His troops could not long hold this position. He mulled over the options. He could pull back, reform and renew the attack. But by this time the Nez Perce had also found cover to hide behind.

He raised his Colt and pulled the trigger, but the hammer fell on an empty chamber. He lowered the weapon, opened the loading gate and inserted new rounds, conscious of his trembling hands.

Department headquarters had warned against unnecessary aggressive action. Israel Damon was convinced he was not going to get caught by the short hair again.

Yet he had been unable to support Colonel Cavanaugh.

Major Damon realized his assignment had really ended in failure.

The sudden explosion of pain in his right side relieved him of the need to think of anything else. He was conscious, too, of the sudden, warm, sticky sensation of his own blood soaking through his shirt. It was the last thing he remembered.

Marcus was with the lead elements of Lemaster's battalion as it struck the edge of the Nez Perce camp, and for a short time he was encouraged to believe their effort would bear fruit. The attack had caught the villagers completely by surprise. Stunned, they stumbled and spilled from their lodges. Some stopped to return the soldiers' fire, while others simply scurried for the nearest available cover.

Marcus felt himself caught up in the exuberance of the moment, controlling his mount with his left hand, firing the big Colt with his right, seeing one warrior buckle and pitch forward. Marcus moved on through the lodges.

Dismounting, he handed the reins of his horse to an orderly and signaled for Johnny Brandt to join him, eyes scanning the unfolding scene, filled with the din and smoke of battle. He had no view of the far end of the village, which was out of sight around the big bend of the Firehole River. Damon should now be moving into action, and if all were proceeding as well on that end the soldiers were in good shape.

The soldiers were squeezing the camp from both ends, but the force from the east had halted its advance and gone on the defensive as the Nez Perce warriors rushed from their tipis and rallied.

"We can send a few warriors to the east to keep the soldiers there busy and use the rest to fight the soldiers at the other end," Little Raven told Bright Sky.

Collecting a handful of warriors, Bright Sky took them to harry Israel Damon's dismounted battalion, while Little Raven moved with the main body of warriors to counter the primary threat from the west.

Across the river, Bright Sky saw soldiers rounding up the pony herd. There would be no survival without horses, he knew, even if they drove back the soldiers. The horses must be recaptured.

Leaving some of the warriors to snipe at Damon's men, Bright Sky took the remainder with him across the river toward the pony herd.

Once they had disposed of the two herd guards, the men of E Company had faced no opposition and were not expecting any as they herded the Nez Perce horses across the now shallow river bed and away from the village.

Bright Sky and his group caught them in mid-passage. Carefully aimed fire felled three troopers in the initial volley, dropping them from their saddles into the shallow water of the Firehole River. Their cavalry mounts joined the Nez Perce ponies, stirrups slapping loosely in their panicked flight.

Surprised by the unexpected resistance, and uncertain as to its origin, E Company was forced to shift its concentration to the attackers. In doing so, they made it possible for the Nez Perce warriors to move in on their horses. Presently E Company found itself embroiled in a smaller version of the larger engagement, battling will-of-the-wisp Nez Perce warriors who seemed to be everywhere and nowhere at the same time.

The Indian resistance, feeble at first, slowly gained in strength. Collecting in small pockets here and there, the warriors resisted from gullies and behind rocks and trees, until eventually their stubborn resistance halted the forward movement of the attackers entirely. They seemed to be concentrating at one end of the camp. Accordingly, as he watched the gradual shift of momentum, Marcus concluded that for whatever reason, Damon had been unable to carry out his assignment. It was the only explanation.

From its furthest point of penetration, Lemaster's battalion was compelled to fall back to a position that afforded at least some cover from the increasingly effective Nez Perce fire that seemed to come at them from all sides.

What had begun as an offensive movement had suddenly turned into a defensive struggle, with the initiative having definitely shifted to the Nez Perce. The Indians had no difficulty locating their target, spread out as it was in a semi-circular position on a small spit of sand, euphemistically called an island, in a now obsolete channel of the old river bed.

Confused by the unexpected turn of events, the cavalrymen were trying to take advantage of the few trees and shrubs their position offered, supplementing them by scooping out rifle pits in the soft sandy soil.

From right to left, Marcus had positioned A Company, followed by C, D and finally, B. The horses of each company were being held on the far end of the island, which meant that with the absence of the horse-holders, each company was reduced in strength by one-fourth, not to mention casualties that now numbered sixteen and growing. Further, a non-commissioned officer and ten troopers from each company had been assigned to remain behind with the pack train at the assembly area. By the time these deductions were accounted for, Marcus found himself with something like one hundred and sixty-three effectives with which to defend what was rapidly becoming an untenable position.

It was already mid-day. The sun was at its apogee and poured its heat down upon the scene below with all the intensity of mid-summer. In the shallow depression some fifty yards behind him, Marcus heard the moans and cries of the wounded begging for water.

Ammunition was running down as well and they were going to need those pack train reserves soon.

"We need water and ammunition, Colonel," Lemaster pointed out.

"I'm aware of that, Captain." A soft thud sounded next to Marcus as a Nez Perce bullet dug into the sandy soil less than a foot away.

"What we need even more is to get out of here or there won't be much need for either water or ammunition," Marcus said.

On the right end of the perimeter, an A Company trooper cried out and pitched forward, adding yet another to the growing list of casualties.

"Get a water party organized, Captain," Marcus directed, and turned to Lieutenant Brandt who had just joined them. "Lieutenant, get word to the company

67

commanders to conserve ammunition. We've got to dig in and hang on 'til dark. Pass the word to the men that we're going to pull out after dark."

"Long day, Colonel," Lemaster said, shaking his head.

"It will be at that," Marcus agreed grimly. "I'm open to suggestions, Captain . . . "

Usually free with both opinions and criticisms, Lemaster was silent.

The water party, half a dozen volunteers carrying all of the canteens they could hold, worked their way toward the main channel of the Firehole River, one hundred yards to the rear of their position, escorted by another half a dozen riflemen. The Nez Perce warriors, knowing full well what the party's mission was, stepped up their harassment fire.

As he surveyed Stephen Lemaster's hard hit battalion, Marcus also found himself pondering the fate of Damon's command. There was no way to know for certain of course, but it seemed likely that Damon might be in equally bad shape. He thought, too, of George Custer and imagined the fate of the Seventh was probably on the mind of more than one man here today.

Traces of powder smoke hung over their position, limpid in the brassy heat. Troopers scrunched down, seeking protection from whatever was available. They swatted the sand fleas that tormented them, cursing the barely visible insects through cracked and swollen lips. Here and there a trooper would raise his carbine and fire, then crouch down to reload from his dwindling supply of cartridges.

The hunters had became the hunted.

Simon Oliver knelt down next to Israel Damon on one knee. The major's features were sallow; he was feverish

68

and his breathing was irregular. He had flirted with consciousness on and off for the past four hours. At the moment he seemed conscious.

Oliver had seen many such wounds and few recovered. He did not believe Israel Damon would prove the exception. Nevertheless, he tried to express optimism when he spoke.

"We're gonna get ourselves outa here, Major."

Damon opened his eyes and tried to focus on the voice. The pain in his body was constant and he was desperately thirsty.

"Water," he croaked softly.

Simon shook his head. "Got none to give, Major. It's for sure why we gotta pull out."

The scout found it tough to find compassion for this man. The major was after all, the victim of his own stupidity. Simon still failed to understand why their attack had been halted. There was no good reason for it at all, and what had it done to Marcus and Lemaster?

Bright Sky and his Nez Perce were making them all look like a bunch of fools. In a sense, it didn't surprise him. He'd long ago lost most of his respect for the army way of thinking, although he regarded Marcus Cavanaugh as an exception.

Captain Pat Foster, F Company's commander and senior captain of the battalion, joined them. He knelt to speak to Major Damon.

"I've assumed command, Major. We're getting cut up here pretty good and I've ordered the men to pull out. E will cover the withdrawal. We'll try to make it as easy on you as possible, but I'm afraid it's going to be a bit uncomfortable for a while."

Damon nodded weakly. "I'll be fine, Captain. What news of the colonel?"

Foster glanced at Simon. "No word, Major. We figure he's pinned down like us."

"Casualties?" Damon asked.

"Four dead, eleven wounded," Foster answered.

Damon sighed and ran a dry tongue over his feverish lips. The figures around him began to slip out of focus again. For a moment he struggled to maintain consciousness, but lacked both the strength and will to persevere. Quickly he was reclaimed by the vacant limbo from which he'd recently emerged.

Surprisingly, Lemaster's water party managed to accomplish its mission while incurring but a single casualty in the process. The water was distributed to the wounded first, then rationed out to the defenders.

The horses, too, were going to need water soon, Marcus knew. He glanced at the sky and uttered a silent prayer of thanks for relief from the waning sun, whose westering angle projected fingers of shadows across the baked landscape. Within the last hour, the firing had tapered off to spasmadic efforts, frequent enough to remind the men of the Eleventh Cavalry that the enemy was still waiting for them.

From the west, the boom of a 12-pounder mountain howitzer echoed through the late afternoon, announcing the arrival of reinforcements under the command of General Carlton Abrams. The explosion was followed by an air burst over the hills near the beleaguered battalion. In quick succession there were two more bursts. For a moment there was a stunned silence, then a rousing cheer rose from the ranks of the defenders.

Marcus harbored mixed emotions. He was as glad to see General Carlton Abrams and three companies of the Twelfth Cavalry—not to mention the howitzer—as any of his men. On the other hand, there was the sense of frustration and failure over his inability to bring the Nez Perce odyssey to an end.

As the commander in the field, the responsibility was his alone. Now, as he contemplated the damage to his regiment in the dying sunlight of a spent September day, that responsibility held a particularly bitter taste. The damage had been administered at the hands of his old friend, Michael Bright Sky. Not for first time since the affair began, he realized how much was at stake for both of them.

From that moment on, the ties of friendship no longer bound the two men. Somehow, Cavanaugh sensed that Bright Sky had beaten him to that conclusion.

Chapter Nine

The Nez Perce tribe was in motion before darkness had fallen. The people moved quickly, grimly silent as they trudged on, remembering the sudden terror of the attack. And though the attackers had been driven back with heavy losses by the great courage of their warriors, the people had suffered losses.

With pride, Bright Sky watched them as they quietly bore the burden of their struggle for freedom, recalling how they had responded to the attack. It was only after the other soldiers came with their big gun that the warriors were forced back. He was sorry that the leader of the soldiers was his old friend Marcus Cavanaugh, but the future of his people was more important than even friendship.

Little Raven and his warriors had remained behind to insure that the people got away safely. They would maintain enough pressure on the soldiers to hold them back.

Two days later, the band emerged from the valley in

a great natural park carpeted with sun-cured buffalo grass stretched out before them, like an undulating tawny ocean that lapped against the shoreline of distant mountains. The brassy heat of the past two days had given way to coolness. From the far end of the cavalcade of Indians, Bright Sky watched a horseman gallop toward him, a swirl of dust trailing behind the pounding hooves of his fleet mount. Soon, Little Raven reined his Appaloosa to a halt in front of his brother and swung down from the animal's back.

For the first time since their ordeal had begun, Bright Sky noticed the fatigue etched on his brother's face. His deep-set eyes were red-rimmed, and his lean, angular features more noticeably pronounced, reflecting the stress of the past few days.

"The soldiers follow," Raven said.

"It was to be expected," Bright Sky acknowledged. "We can only hope to stay ahead of them long enough for us to reach the Grandmother Land."

"The warriors will see to it," Little Raven vowed. "A hunting party has located a small herd of buffalo," he added.

Bright Sky nodded. "The meat and hides will be put to good use."

As they walked, a silence grew up between them.

"Where are the soldiers?"

"A full sleep behind us, maybe less," Raven said.

Bright Sky nodded. "We have far to travel. The Grandmother Land is ten sleeps, maybe longer. North of the stinking springs the land is not well known to us. The way will be hard. Horsetooth Mountain, I am told, offers a good place to rest, with water, and grass for the horses. From there it is only two sleeps to the Grandmother Land." He paused to let his words take root, before continuing. "We will have to ask more of ourselves than we thought possible, my brother. The soldiers will not stop. More will be sent."

"We will be ready," Raven said.

Bright Sky stopped and placed his hand on Little Raven's shoulder. "I know you are, my brother. Just remember, we cannot afford to waste the courage of a single warrior. There are none to replace those who are killed."

Overhead, the pale wash of blue sky had now deteriorated to a leaden gray. It seemed to Bright Sky that the promise of what lay ahead was as chilling as the raw wind that bore down on them from the northwest.

Five officers sat in General Carlton Abrams' tent, the general, Colonel Marcus Cavanaugh, Captain Stephen Lemaster, Lieutenant John Brandt and Captain Jake Randall, Abrams' adjutant. Each of the men held a steaming cup of coffee and each relished the heat put forth by the small conical Sibley stove.

"Marcus, this thing's gotten out of hand," General Abrams thundered. "Forty-eight hours ago we were on the verge of wrapping this thing up. Now look at us! Whipped, Marcus! Whipped by a bunch of damn . . . "

"By a bunch of damn good fighters, General," Marcus interjected.

Carlton Abrams ignored the remark and continued. "Washington is already unhappy, Marcus. Sherman can't understand why it's taking so bloody long. When he hears about the Firehole he'll really be on his ear."

Marcus sighed. "Yes, sir. With the greatest respect, I might suggest that if General Sherman doesn't understand what's going on, he come out here and get educated."

Carlton Abrams shot a sharp glance at his colonel, then softened his expression somewhat. "I know, I know, Marcus. No headquarters commander ever appreciates the problems of his field commanders."

The general paused to sip his coffee, then added, "And I suspect the reverse of that is also true. It may surprise you to know that General Sherman is in fact in this part of country. He's vacationing in Yellowstone Park."

Marcus looked up.

The general permitted himself the luxury of a brief grin. "I can also tell you that Washington does have some appreciation of the situation. Jake, let's have that map." Carlton turned to his adjutant, who unrolled the area map, laying it out on the small writing desk in front of the general. Abrams studied it for a moment, then pointed a finger at their approximate position.

"Colonel Norris is organizing a column at Fort Starke with orders to move as soon as we have some idea as to where these devils are headed. Any ideas about that, Marcus?"

"Well, it's just a hunch right now, General."

"Oh come, Marcus, this is no time for modesty. Let's have it."

"General, my hunch is that the Nez Perce are heading for Canada. I think we'll see them turn north before long. Bright Sky knows about Sitting Bull, and it's my hunch he'll look for a refuge in the same place."

Carlton Abrams twirled an unlit cigar around in his mouth, studying the map before him. "It makes sense, Marcus. And I'm going to gamble that you're right. I'll direct Maynard Norris to act accordingly. I'm also going to order Major Taylor to move down from the north. He doesn't have much to spare up there at Fort Lewis, but if he can manage to get even a small column in front of the Nez Perce it just might slow them down enough to bring you within range."

Mad Maynard Norris, Marcus thought, remembering the Civil War reputation of the colonel, whose stature had been second only to that of George Custer. "Mad" the press had dubbed him for his propensity to attack nearly any position. How many lives, Marcus wondered, had been the price of that reputation?

"This will give us three columns in the field, Marcus," Abrams continued. "I want to emphasize how serious Washington is about all this. The Nez Perce must be caught. For them to reach Canada is politically unthinkable. And of course I needn't remind you what that means to professional soldiers like you and me if the politicians get hold of it."

"Understood, sir."

Carlton Abrams got to his feet. "I sincerely hope so, Marcus, for both our sakes. I've got to get back to headquarters. I trust that if I leave you three companies of the Twelfth, you can spare me a small escort."

"I think it can be arranged, General."

"Good. Oh and by the way, Marcus, take those damn civilians with you," Abrams growled under his breath.

"Is that a direct order?"

"Yes, dammit, Colonel. I don't like it any better than you do!"

"Yes, sir," Marcus said, rising. "Officers call fifteen minutes, John," he told Lieutenant Brandt. Turning, he saluted General Abrams. "I'll keep you informed of developments, General."

Carlton Abrams nodded. "I do appreciate the problem with this assignment, Marcus, believe me. I know the Eleventh got cut up pretty good at the Firehole River, but you're going to have to press this thing through to the end. Let's hope the job can be finished quickly. Better for everyone."

"Except maybe the Nez Perce," Marcus added, half aloud.

"Especially the Nez Perce," Abrams replied. "Good hunting, Marcus." He extended his hand.

"Thank you, sir." Marcus Cavanaugh accepted the outstretched hand of his department commander, aware of the sincerity in the older man's grasp. He started out of the tent, followed by Brandt and Lemaster.

"Oh, Marcus," Abrams said. "One last thing."

Marcus waved Brandt and Lemaster on ahead.

"The Damon thing is regrettable. How is he?"

"Alive, sir, but barely."

Abrams nodded. "Poor devil. Anyway, whatever action you plan to take will have to wait until this thing with the Nez Perce is cleared up."

"Understood, General." Marcus stepped outside into the morning chill. Lemaster and Brandt were waiting for him.

Culled of its casualties the regiment was in motion by noon. Following a brief service, the dead were buried and an ambulance train was organized to take the wounded to a civilian hospital at Junction City, sixty miles distant.

Marcus paid a visit to the hospital before the column pulled out. Israel Damon, he found, was still unconscious. He didn't seem any worse, but there wasn't any particular reason to be optimistic about the man's chances for recovery. Should the major somehow manage to beat the odds and survive, Marcus decided he would prefer charges. He disliked the idea, but concluded it was one of those distasteful tasks a commander had to face from time to time. Command responsibility touched the lives of too many to be taken lightly.

Later, in a rare moment of privacy, he reached into his breast pocket and withdrew a letter from Elizabeth. The letter was posted nearly three weeks ago and had arrived with the general's party. This was the first opportunity he'd had to look at it.

Opening the letter, the sweet scent that emerged seemed strangely out of place in the harshness of his immediate surroundings. And yet he found himself stirred by the memories it evoked.

Dear Marcus:

I have no idea as to where this may find you, if it does at all. In the hope that it does reach you, I wanted to express again my warm personal thanks for a marvelous summer at Fort Casey. I shall treasure it always.

The Nez Perce incident is most unfortunate, and I pray the matter will be settled quickly and painlessly.

I should be greatly disappointed if you failed to call on me when next you are in New York.
Fondly,
Elizabeth

He read the letter a second time, then carefully folded and returned it to his pocket, feeling at once elevated and disturbed by her remarks. She had not been far from the forefront of his thoughts since the last night at Fort Casey. Indeed, in those rare moments of late, when not preoccupied with the Nez Perce business, he found himself thinking frequently of her and it troubled him. For two decades, the army had been his mistress, and he had been faithful. Was a triangle developing, he wondered? The question was both intriguing and unsettling.

*   *   *

By late afternoon, the regiment was pushing hard on the Nez Perce trail. The three companies of the Twelfth Cavalry, along with the howitzer, had been recalled by General Abrams, leaving Marcus with eight understrength companies to continue the pursuit. Having learned a bitter lesson, Marcus now had detachments sweeping the country ahead and along both flanks. Finally, a small trailing squad covered the rear of the column, a mile or more behind the pack train.

As chief scout, Simon Oliver ranged far out ahead of the column with a small detachment. On two separate occasions, Oliver's men were fired on by the Nez Perce rear guard, but suffered no casualties. Likewise, the scouts were unable to inflict any damage on the Nez Perce.

In camp that evening, Marcus listened to the scout's report, nursing a cup of coffee in the process.

"They 'pear to be headin' toward the park," Oliver said, referring to the recently created Yellowstone National Park, a mysterious area filled with great natural wonders it was said. It had just been named the nation's first national park.

"How far ahead?"

"Main party is maybe two days, but the warriors are closer," the scout estimated.

Marcus sighed. "Well, again they've got the jump on us and we've got some ground to cover, Simon."

"Won't be easy, Marcus, 'specially in the park. I don't know that stretch of country real well, but from what I do know it will be tough to make up much ground 'til they swing north—assuming your hunch about them headin'for Canada is right, that is."

Marcus looked at him. "Which reminds me, you haven't said what you thought they might be up to."

Simon Oliver got slowly to his feet, yawned and stretched. "I think you pegged it right on the head, Marcus. Right on the head."

Marcus finished the last of his coffee. "Well, it would seem we have a meeting of the minds, Simon."

The scout nodded. "So it would seem."

"I'm going to steal a march on Bright Sky," Marcus announced. "See if we can't cut down that distance a bit. We stand to horse at midnight, John. Pass the word."

Simon Oliver finished his coffee. "Another night march. Just what I was hopin' for."

Chapter Ten

Little Raven and five other warriors watched in interested silence from the edge of the timber as a six-horse stagecoach braked to a halt and disgorged its passengers. Six civilian sightseers alighted from the stagecoach. Stretching and yawning they looked at the rough-hewn log structure that served as a stage station and were duly unimpresssed. It was, however, a glorious day and the stunning beauty of the immediate surroundings more than offset the drabness of the station.

The three female members of the party excused themselves and walked toward the station. A gangling youth emerged from the station and proceeded to unhitch the stage team and replace it with fresh animals.

The party was returning to Salt Lake City, having journeyed north to view the reputed wonders of the the nation's first national park. It had been an exhilarating experience. Yellowstone had proven to be a spectacle far exceeding their imaginations.

It was the youngest man of the group, Charles Fitzgerald, who first noticed a mounted Indian watching him as he relieved himself in the bushes. He recovered his composure and stumbled back toward his companions. By the time he reached them, a dozen other braves had joined the first observer, forming a semi-circle at the edge of the timber fifty yards from the station.

The women emerged from the station, chatting and giggling, having failed to notice what had captured the men's attention. Presently, one did. Gasping, she made her companions aware of the visitors.

The manager of the station came out, eyeballed the situation, scratched his balding head and studied the line of motionless Indians. They sat on their ponies impassively, carbine butts resting on bronzed thighs.

"What do they want?" Fitzgerald asked.

"Hanged if I know," the station manager answered. "Who kin ever tell 'bout an Injun? Probably want whiskey."

The Indians moved slowly toward the station. Surrounding the little party, they stared down at the increasingly nervous tourists.

"What you want?" The station manager asked, using halting sign talk.

The Indians remained expressionless and silent. At length, Little Raven pointed to the sightseers with a sweeping motion of his index finger.

"You will come with us," he commanded in a voice that would brook no suggestions otherwise.

Despite her fear, Kathleen Fitzgerald, Charles's wife, thought Little Raven a handsome specimen of manhood. Strong aquiline features framed the blackest pair of eyes she'd ever seen.

"Now wait . . . " The station manager never finished his protest. The butt of the big Sharps rifle dropped him senseless to the earth like a pole-axed steer. One of the women screamed, then fainted. The men stood ashen-faced.

Little Raven motioned for the whites to climb up behind a warrior. Those warriors without a passenger amused themselves by climbing aboard the stagecoach, examining every nook and cranny. Then they rocked it back and forth, until it tipped completely over, to the howling delight of the playful Nez Perce warriors.

Presently, the leader signaled an end to the frivolous antics and the group trotted off with their prisoners in tow.

Bright Sky watched the riders come into camp, saw the travel beaten passengers and the terror in their eyes as they looked around at the wandering village and its inhabitants.

"Who are these people and why have you brought them here?" he asked Raven sharply.

"The soldiers will not dare attack us while they are here," Little Raven said, gesturing toward the six hostages.

Bright Sky watched his people gathering around the visitors. There was some truth to what Raven said, and yet he sensed this was not good. "We will talk of this more. In the meantime, these people must be treated kindly."

Later, Bright Sky, Little Raven, Elk and Black Dove sat around the fire. Swan served them food and retired to a corner of the lodge, which was one of the few remaining in the village since the soldier attack at the Firehole River. Bright Sky harbored a sense of guilt that he should have a warm lodge while so many were without. But Swan and Little Raven persuaded him that it was fitting and proper and so he had accepted.

"These people will protect us from the soldiers," Little Raven persisted, as the topic of discussion moved quickly to that of the captives. "The soldiers will not dare attack while these whites are here."

Black Dove shook his head. "This was not a good thing to do, Raven. It will not keep the soldiers away and it will go harder on us if the captives are here when the soldiers do come."

Bright Sky held up his hand, asking for silence. "There is truth to what each of you says. It is too late to worry now about whether it was a good thing to take the whites. Shall we keep them, as my brother argues, or send them away?"

One by one, each decided there was some advantage in keeping the hostages. If nothing else, perhaps they could be used to buy freedom later on. Bright Sky was uncomfortable with the decision, but had no choice except to honor a clear consensus.

"Very well," he agreed. "We will keep them with us for the time being, but they must be treated with kindness above all. To do otherwise is to invite the wrath of the soldiers."

The others nodded, agreeing with Bright Sky's reasoning.

"Bring their leader to me," Bright Sky said. "I will speak with him."

Moments later, the spokesman of the party, an obviously uneasy young man was ushered into the lodge. Bright Sky motioned him to a seat across the fire.

"What is your name?"

"Carver. Michael Carver," the man said.

Bright Sky smiled. "Michael is my name also. My Christian name. It was given to me when I attended the mission school many years ago."

Michael Carver forced a smile that felt as weak as it

looked. He tried to speak but the words caught in his throat.

"Have you had food?"

Carver nodded.

Bright Sky smiled. "You will not be harmed unless you try something foolish. We have decided you should remain with us for a time."

"But we have families," Carver pointed out, suddenly finding some emotion to accompany his voice.

"And you shall see them again, Mr. Carver. But for now you and the others must understand that it is necessary for you to travel with us. We will try and make you as comfortable as possible, but please remember this is a difficult time for us."

Sensing the discussion was ended, Michael Carver got to his feet and stepped out, escorted by one of Little Raven's warriors. Bright Sky hoped their decision was the right one.

Marcus pushed the regiment through the light but steady rain that had been falling for the past thirty-six hours. He was certain there wasn't a dry piece of equipment anywhere in the column.

The strain of the campaign had begun to tell on the horses, too. A few had already pulled up lame and these were being herded along with the pack train, their riders relegated to the role of foot soldiers. Marcus imagined he was likely to have a sizeable infantry contingent under his command before this was finished.

He tilted his head upward, hoping to see some suggestion of relief from the prevailing soggy conditions, but saw nothing to encourage such hope. Water dripped from the brim of his sodden campaign hat onto his face, though he scarcely noticed it. He signaled a halt, then ordered the march resumed on foot for half an hour, to conserve the horses.

At noon he ordered a brief halt and allowed the men to build small coffee fires, providing of course they could locate anything dry enough to burn.

His dog robber, a leathery-faced veteran named Ames, had managed to get a fire started and had coffee water boiling almost before Marcus was ready.

Marcus sat on a huge off-trail deadfall, beneath a small lean-to that served as a temporary regimental headquarters. Holding a tin of steaming coffee, he listened to the reports of his company commanders. Tired, wet and hungry, their voices were edged with irritability. They had lost two days getting reorganized after the battle at Firehole River, making arrangements for the removal of wounded and waiting for a supply train to arrive. All the while, Bright Sky had pushed on and was now, by their best reckoning, three days ahead.

"Gentlemen, it's been a frustrating campaign thus far," Marcus offered. "But keep in mind that it hasn't exactly been easy on the Nez Perce, either."

Simon Oliver slipped in under the lean-to and and squatted down, pouring himself a tin of coffee. When he'd taken a satisfying sip, he looked up at Marcus.

"Well?" Marcus asked.

"Well, they've definitely turned north, so it appears your hunch is right, Marcus."

Marcus picked up the map at his side and opened it up. "Lay it out for us."

The scout hunched forward, stuck his index finger on a small section of the map marked Yellowstone Park, and moved the finger up, in a general northerly direction.

"They turned north out of the park somewhere

86

about here. My guess is they'll head for Burnt Meadows. Real good chance of findin' buffalo there."

"How far, Simon?"

"A day for them, four for us."

Marcus frowned.

"Might be a way to cut that down, Marcus."

"I'm all ears, Simon."

"It's like this, Marcus," Simon said, pointing to a thin line on the map. "Here's our position and where I figure they are. Now, if we was to go like so," he said, gesturing with the edge of his hand, diagonally across the map, "I figure we'd save one day and that might be enough to catch Bright Sky before he leaves Burnt Meadows."

Marcus studied the map for a moment, then looked up at Simon. "Another up and over march. And no guarantees."

"That's about it, Marcus."

"Well, I don't see we have much choice. Let's hope Bright Sky decides to take an extra day's rest, which I doubt. But then maybe our luck's changing."

Marcus gave them an hour, at the end of which they were in the saddle once again, pushing through a drizzle that seemed to have recovered some of its lost vigor.

"That colonel of yours must have sheet iron in his britches to spend so much time in the saddle," a grizzled trooper said to Ames as they rode through the wet, drab afternoon. "By Christ, Ames, I tell you my ass ain't never been so sore, not to mention my knees and legs."

Theobald Ames looked at the trooper and smiled. The man was a good soldier. He griped a lot. "The colonel knows what has to be done," Ames explained patiently.

"I sure as hell hope so," the trooper grumbled. "I

for one could use some whiskey, a woman and a bit of hot food, in that order."

Marcus pushed them on into the early evening, through an intermittent rain that seemed unable to choose between mist and hard drizzle. They halted at eight, rested four hours, and moved on just after midnight. The horses were tired, Marcus knew, and so were the men, but this was one of those times when men and animals were asked to give beyond what they thought themselves capable of. It was true of himself and no less true of others.

The country through which Simon guided them was cut with swales and rough ridges, pocked with cedar and oak. The mountains Simon had spoken of were not as high and lofty as those the troops crossed a few days ago, but what they lacked in elevation they more than made up for in treacherous footing.

By noon of the third day, they were within five miles of Burnt Meadows. Horses and men showed the effects of the driving march, but if it resulted in putting an end to the whole business it would be worth it in the long run. For now, he ordered the horses unsaddled, fed and rubbed down. The men were allowed small fires and a chance for some sleep, while the indefatigable Simon Oliver went on ahead to scout the Nez Perce camp. When he returned three hours later, Marcus assembled the officers.

"Lady luck is with us, Marcus. They're still there."

Marcus nodded. "Good. We'll attack at first light. F Company will have the advance. If there are no questions, get some sleep, gentlemen."

Anson Demarest edged his way to the front of the group, a sodden unlit cigar stub projecting from the corner of his mouth. "My boys don't figure to be shoved aside this time, Colonel."

Marcus glared at him, suppressing an urge to have the man thrown out of camp. "You will carry out your orders just like anyone else in this command, Mr. Demarest. Do I make myself clear?"

Anson Demarest removed the cigar stub from his mouth and spat arrogantly to one side. "Why 'course, Colonel," he said, a sardonic smile spreading across his pouchy, unshaven features. "Only like I say, us volunteers didn't come all this way to set around twiddlin' our thumbs."

Again, Marcus stifled an urge to have the man arrested and the volunteers ordered back, General Abrams' orders notwithstanding. However, for the moment at least, he would have to put up with the man. His troops could ill-afford a confrontation with the volunteers right now. It would have to wait.

Foster's F Company took the lead, followed by E, G and H and the volunteers. Lemaster's battalion, with the pack train, trailed as a reserve. Marcus rode with Simon Oliver, Lieutenant Brandt and a small detachment well ahead of Foster's lead company.

At the base of a low ridge, Simon signaled a halt. Dismounting, he wormed his way to the crest and peered over, returning at length to where Marcus and the others waited.

"Still there?" Marcus asked.

Oliver nodded. "Sizeable bunch of warriors. Rear guard's all I can figure. Main village must be up ahead. There's a small creek about three hundred yards the other side of this ridge. No cover between here and there, so you'll need to make it quick, Marcus, 'cause they'll scatter in a hurry."

Thirty minutes later, with Foster's battalion on hand, Marcus issued the attack assignments. Foster, with his own and E Company, would attack head-on, while G and H Companies would strike from the right flank. Demarest's volunteers had been assigned to support G and H Companies on the right, and now moved off in that direction. Marcus would remain with Foster's unit.

The rain, which had actually ceased for several hours, resumed as a steady drizzle again, signaling that the developing day offered nothing better than the somber gray skies of its predecessor.

Foster's squadron assembled at the base of the ridge, sitting silent in the drizzle, waiting the allotted thirty minutes for the flanking companies to get into position. Suddenly, from that direction came the sound of firing. It was too soon, Marcus knew, but there was no time to worry about that now. He gave the signal and Foster's squadron moved up the shallow slope. In another moment they were surging down and across the soggy expanse of Burnt Meadows.

As Foster's squadron bore down on the encampment of Nez Perce warriors, it was clear that the attack from the right had been premature, and Marcus suspected the volunteers. Consequently, the Nez Perce had just enough warning to disperse and take cover. They were able to meet Foster's arrival with enough strength to empty a few saddles, and force the charging troopers to dismount and form a skirmish line.

Working their Springfields, the troopers pushed forward, but progress was slow. For the second time, the Nez Perce resistance seemed equal to the challenge, in this case probably aided by the premature attack on the part of the volunteers.

Marcus saw a young lieutenant in Foster's company clutch his shoulder and pitch forward. Lining up his Colt, Marcus fired. He felt the jump of the big handgun and saw a Nez Perce warrior spin and fall to the ground.

On the right flank, G and H Companies were pressing forward as well. Despite the presence of the volunteers, who now seemed more vocal than anything else, they were making progress. But the trap had been sprung, giving the warriors a chance to melt back into the nearby timber.

Marcus waas angry because the campaign continued to be frustrating. Nevertheless he derived some consolation from the fact that they had at least captured a few supplies, not to mention the horses that could be used to replace those of his own that were unserviceable.

Marcus directed Foster's company to pressure the warriors and locate the main village, while he moved up to support with the rest of the regiment.

"Go with him, Simon," he said to the scout.

Oliver nodded. "You sure you don't want me to take Demarest and his boys, too, Marcus?"

"I'd like nothing better, Simon."

"Figured so," the scout replied.

"See what you can find for us. Bright Sky can't be that far ahead. We'll not be more than a couple of hours behind you."

"I'll do what I can, Marcus."

Marcus turned to Pat Foster. "Captain, when and if you locate the Nez Perce, your job is to hang on 'til the rest of us get here. Don't try and do the whole thing yourself. Understood?"

"Understood, Colonel." He saluted and moved out to the head of his column, Simon Oliver at his side. Marcus watched him move off. The rain had picked up and now came down with renewed intensity.

Chapter Eleven

Although the young Nez Perce warrior was barely conscious, he was alert enough to feel the excruciating pain caused by the big Sharps slug that had torn a hole in his right thigh. Unable to leave with the other braves, he had hidden, only to be discovered by two volunteers. They dragged him back to camp where they received the plaudits of their comrades, many of whom had already begun to celebrate the day's victory.

The warrior's wrists were lashed with rawhide, his arms extended full length and tied between two trees, suspended just enough for the weight of his body to increase the pain in the wounded limb. Several times he passed out, only to be revived by his captors.

"I allow we ought to cut that leg off," one of the volunteers declared in a whiskey-slurred voice.

"Go ahead, Clell," a voice from the crowd encouraged.

"Shit, Clell, you ain't got the guts!" another taunted.

92

"Damn," Clell growled. "I'll show you." He started toward the warrior, knife in hand.

"Drop it!" the voice was flat and ugly. "I said drop it!"

Clell turned to see Lieutenant Johnny Brandt standing behind him with Simon Oliver on his right.

"You heard the lieutenant, friend. I'd be real prompt was I you," Simon added.

Something in the grim tone of the scout's voice carried the necessary persuasion. Clell paused for a moment, sheathed his knife and backed down. Simon and Brandt walked up and cut the warrior's bonds. They eased him down, placing his arms around their shoulders, and took him away for medical attention.

"I want you and your people out of here by morning, Mr. Demarest," Marcus Cavanaugh said, facing the leader of the volunteers.

"Not by a damn sight, Colonel. We got us a stake in this thing."

"I'm afraid you don't understand, Demarest. You don't have a choice. Either you and your men pack up and head back, or I'll have you and any others who object placed under arrest and escorted back to Fort Casey."

"You gonna get yourself in more trouble 'n you can handle, you try that, soldier boy." Demarest said it flat and ugly.

"If I was you, I'd let it end right there."

Anson Demarest looked into the steady gaze of the most penetrating pair of eyes he'd ever seen, spat off to one side and decided maybe the bluff wasn't worth calling.

"You ain't heard the last of this, Cavanaugh. Mark my words!"

"By morning, Demarest," Marcus reiterated. "Early morning."

"My guess is you can expect to hear about that from General Abrams," John Brandt predicted, watching Demarest shuffle off.

"You can bet on that," Marcus agreed. "Comes with the job, Johnny. You may have a new boss before this is over, but in the meantime we've got a job to do and those volunteers are more liability than asset. Particularly when they start torturing Indian prisoners. Pass the word. We move at first light."

In the descending twilight, the drizzle that had soaked the country the past two days continued its relentless work. Marcus went into the tent Ames had erected, lit a candle and made a brief entry in his journal.

"Coffee, Colonel?" Ames asked, handing him a cup of steaming blackness.

"Thank you, Ames." He leaned back against his McClellan saddle, conscious suddenly of the great fatigue that had taken command of his body. He felt the hot coffee coursing through his system and wished he had something stronger to flavor it with.

"Excuse me, Colonel . . . "

Marcus looked up and saw Brandt standing alone. "Courier from headquarters." He handed Marcus a dispatch. Marcus opened the pouch and removed the message.

Be advised that Nez Perce captured six white hostages in Yellowstone Park. Present condition unknown. Take all precautions for safety of hostages.
C. Abrams
Brig. Gen' Commd'g. Dept.

94

Marcus handed the dispatch to Brandt who read it and shook his head. "Just what we need, Colonel. Another complication."

Marcus nodded. "Get rid of one and another shows up."

"Any response, sir?"

Marcus shook his head. "Just acknowledge receipt of the message."

Brandt scribbled a note to the courier, telling him to get some food and sleep before starting back. Then he turned back to Marcus. "A change in plans, Colonel?"

"Have the company commanders join me here in fifteen minutes, John."

Marcus had Ames build up the small fire and thought about what their approach ought to be now, knowing the Nez Perce held six white hostages. This kind of action would cost the Nez Perce whatever sympathy they might otherwise have had. He wondered if Bright Sky had considered the consequences?

"Well, gentlemen, this does complicate our life," Marcus said after the company commanders had been briefed. "It means that Bright Sky has an advantage he didn't have before. We simply can't afford to take unnecessary risks with those hostages."

"What in hell were they doing in a place like that anyway?" Stephen Lemaster grumbled.

"Little too late to worry about that, Captain," Marcus said.

"You think Bright Sky would really harm those hostages, Colonel?"

Marcus shook his head. "Not ordinarily, but this is not an ordinary situation. Despite what it may seem like

95

from here, the Nez Perce are in a noose and it's getting tighter. When survival's at stake anything can happen."

"What's the plan then, Colonel?" Lemaster asked.

"No change. We march at three a.m. and deal with the situation as it develops. For now, keep those hostages in mind should you find yourselves in a position that calls for independent action. Now if there are no more questions, I propose to get some sleep, gentlemen, and suggest you do the same.

When they'd gone, Marcus stretched out, covering himself with the single blanket. His body was tired and yearned for sleep, while his mind, awash with thoughts, wrestled with the Nez Perce issue. He found himself wondering whether Bright Sky was struggling with the same problem. It was curious how two men from such fundamentally different cultures could find themselves grappling with the same problem, each from a different perspective. When it came at length, the sleep was restless and troubled.

Sometime during the night, the rain ceased at last and when Ames awakened Cavanaugh, a ribbon of pink was just beginning to edge the eastern horizon. He arose, feeling stiff and groggy, as though he'd not slept at all. Ames handed him a cup of coffee, which he savored in the damp chill, taking a moment to reflect on how it seemed to take longer to work out the kinks on mornings such as this. He recalled a time in his younger days when he would scarcely have noticed the stiffness and fatigue.

The regiment moved out a half hour later, just as a splendid sunrise got underway, flooding the east with brilliant orange.

At mid-day a courier from Foster's company reported in with a message that Foster was on the Nez Perce trail, apparently half a day ahead. He had had a brush with the warriors, but not wanting to exceed his orders, he didn't force the issue or attempt to close in on the Nez Perce camp itself.

Marcus sent the courier back with an order to maintain surveillance but take no action until the regiment came up.

The regiment linked up with Foster late that afternoon, at which time Marcus briefed Foster and Simon Oliver on the hostage situation.

The scout whistled softly. "Well, that does complicate things just a bit, Marcus. How do you propose to handle it?"

Marcus took a long pull of the tepid water in his canteen, swished it around in his mouth and spat it out. "Got any of that coffee of yours left, Ames?" Ames disappeared.

A moment later Ames appeared, handed the colonel a tin of coffee and disappeared again. Marcus took a sip, then looked up to meet Simon Oliver's steady gaze.

"You and I are going to ride into that Nez Perce camp under a flag of truce and see if we can negotiate with Bright Sky for the release of those hostages."

"You shore put a lot of faith in a piece of white cloth, Marcus. I'm not that confident about it, not where my life's on the line."

"My confidence is in Bright Sky," Marcus said. "He's a reasonable man. I think I can talk to him on reasonable terms."

"I dunno, Marcus. Depends on how much influence he still has, or whether Little Raven's callin' the shots."

"We'll have to find that out, Simon. Of course I can't force you to go with me."

The scout looked at Marcus. "I'd never forgive myself if anything happened to you, Marcus."

"Ames," the scout called out. "I better have some

of whatever that is the Colonel's drinkin'. Maybe it'll affect me the same way."

Kathleen Fitzgerald had cried often since her abduction by the heathen Indians. Already it seemed forever, though in fact it was only a few days. Somewhere she had heard or read that Indians never cried or displayed emotion, and so she'd had presence of mind to restrict her tears to those moments when her captors were not around. She also felt dirty and unkempt. If she survived this ordeal, she vowed to never let a day pass without bathing.

Her companions were equally distraught. Her brother and sister-in-law, Ben and Elaine Johnson, whose idea it had been to visit Yellowstone Park in the first place, were moody and uncommunicative, which both surprised and disappointed her. She had expected a stronger reaction from her brother. She had never really liked her sister-in-law anyway, so Elaine's behavior was more in the nature of suspicions confirmed.

A friend of Kathleen's husband, Michael Carver, had accompanied them, and Elaine Johnson had brought along her younger sister, Marcy, who seemed to bear up surprisingly well, especially compared to her companions. Kathleen attributed it to the girl's youthful curiosity. At the age of fifteen there was little that escaped her questioning scrutiny. While the others were fearful for their very existence, Marcy seemed intrigued by the surroundings of her captors. Their every movement appeared to fascinate her. Where the others gagged at the thought of eating boiled dog, for example, Marcy approached it as a unique opportunity.

At the moment her companions were sleeping, which afforded Kathleen an opportunity to collect her wits and reflect a bit on their situation. It was nearing dawn.

Crawling forward, she carefully drew back a corner of the tipi flap to peer outside. The faintest streak of pink was breeching the eastern horizon. Wrapping herself in a blanket, she stepped outside.

How long he stood there behind her she had no idea. She only knew that suddenly she sensed a presence, and turned to see him standing there. She thought he was the leader. She had to admit he was an imposing figure, with a kind of dignity she would not have expected to find in a heathen.

Startled, she would have cried out had it not been for his outstretched hand which conveyed his peaceful intent. He had a benevolent look on his lined, broad face. She found herself unafraid and at ease in his presence.

He squatted down across from her. "My name is Michael Bright Sky, young lady. It would please me to know your name."

"You speak . . . "

"English." Bright Sky finished the question. "Yes. My brother and I both attended mission school as children for several years. We are not uneducated savages, Miss . . . "

"Fitzgerald, Kathleen Fitzgerald," she stammered, adding, "Why are you holding us prisoner? We have done nothing to you."

He nodded. "True. And I regret the necessity of doing this. But my people have come far and our journey is a long way from over. Your soldiers come after us and they will not stop until we are back on the reservation where we cannot survive. With you here the soldiers will not be so quick to attack. I promise no harm shall come to you while you are with us."

"But we have families . . . " she started to say, before Bright Sky waved her to silence.

"I am sorry, but this is something that must be," he said, rising. "Perhaps it will be a good thing for you to see how it truly is with us." He pointed at the tipi where the rest of the hostages were sleeping and smiled quickly. "The young girl," he said, "she learns much. You would all do well to follow her example."

"But how long do you plan to hold us? Do you think it is fair to keep us as prisoners . . . ?"

A sad smile crossed his wide, sensuous mouth. "Fair, Kathleen Fitzgerald? What is truly fair? Is it fair that we be prisoners on our reservation while the whites slowly steal our land? Is it fair for the soldiers to come after us like animals?" He shook his head slowly. "I do not know how long. Until we reach the safety of the Grand-mother Land."

"Where is that?" she asked.

"Canada," he replied. "And now I must leave. Please remember, no harm will come to any of you—unless of course you do something foolish." He turned and walked into the gray light of dawn.

Reflecting on what she had been told, Katherine went back inside the tipi and lay down, feeling more relaxed than she'd felt since their abduction. The noise of the others moving around awoke her an hour later. She said nothing to the others of Bright Sky's visit, and began combing her long dark hair.

"You seem content enough this morning," Marcy observed, "preening yourself like a peacock. You been courtin' with one of our captors?"

Kathleen felt herself blush. There was no way Marcy could have known of Bright Sky's visit unless she had not been asleep. But Kathleen was certain she had been. It was simply the girl's natural inclination to see something romantic in every situation.

Kathleen swung her head in a flourish and stood up.

"I'm tired of being dirty and feeling unwashed," she declared. "I'm going down to the river and take a bath."

"Kathleen!" her husband Charles said, horrified. "I'll not permit it."

"Well, I don't know how you'll stop it, Charles," she said, with a tone of determination he'd never heard her use before.

"I believe I'll do the same," Marcy announced. She stalked after Kathleen.

"Well, I'll not be the only unclean lady in this group," Elaine uttered and followed the first two, leaving in their wake three confused and puzzled males.

Chapter Twelve

Behind the wandering tribe of Nez Perce Indians lay the relentless, eastward flowing waters of the Yellowstone River. The Indians had crossed the river at mid-day and pushed on, reaching their present position along a small creek as the sun faded behind a low-lying cloud bank to the west.

It had been a long, arduous day. Indeed, each passing day drained the tribe a little more of it's vitality. Now, watching the tired bodies as they moved through the motions of establishing a camp of sorts, Bright Sky thought of the journey that remained and wondered if they would make it.

Food was also beginning to run low, burdening him with yet another concern. They had seen no buffalo in several days, although old signs were occasionally seen. Blankets, robes, and warm clothing had been on his mind as well. This day had been ripe with the warmth of early autumn, but they could expect few such days in the future.

The journey itself was difficult enough, made all the more so because of the soldiers. One never knew from which direction they might come, the vigilance of the warriors notwithstanding. Yesterday, Raven's braves had been surprised by yet another column of soldiers moving toward the Yellowstone River.

The fighting had been harsh, but the soldiers were too few in number to cause a serious problem and were soon driven off. However, each encounter bled a little more life out of the people, and yesterday was no exception, having resulted in the death of three more warriors. Despite the growing gaps in their ranks, the jubilant warriors were coming to regard themselves as somewhat invincible. After all, hadn't each encounter with the blue-coats found them triumphant?

Bright Sky, though pleased with their success, was nevertheless troubled by this attitude. To a far greater extent than most of his people, he understood the power that the white man could bring to bear. He realized that the one advantage they had was to move quickly before that power was concentrated against them. Once that happened, they would have no chance.

There would be time enough for jubilation when they reached the Grandmother Land. But right now, Marcus Cavanaugh was behind them.

Little Raven rode up beside Bright Sky and dismounted. Together they stood in silence for a time, watching the camp take shape in the waning afternoon.

"I sense a sadness in you," Raven said at length.

"I think of those who died yesterday fighting the soldiers."

Little Raven looked away, feeling the same sense of loss. Each time they fought there were a few who did not return. But how could they hope to gain their freedom without losing some in the process. The logic worked, but did not satisfy the hunger of loss.

"I, too, feel that loss, but there is no other way," Little Raven said, pausing for a moment before continuing. "Besides the soldiers, we have another problem."

Bright Sky looked at him questioningly.

"Powder and bullets are beginning to run low."

Bright Sky nodded. "Then we must find more. We cannot expect to reach the Grandmother Land without fighting more soldiers, and more bullets will be needed if we are to do that."

"I have been thinking about this," the younger man said after a time. "There may be a way."

Bright Sky watched him carefully, wondering what his resourceful younger brother was going to produce in the way of an idea.

"There is a place, maybe two days from here, where the soldiers have supplies of ammunition, food, blankets. It is on an island in the Missouri River. The big boats stop there and unload supplies, which are then taken to the forts."

Bright Sky had heard of the place. It was called Antelope Island.

"Only a few soldiers guard the place. We could capture it and have all of the supplies we need for the rest of our journey."

Bright Sky pondered the plan. There seemed no better way for them to get supplies that would be sorely needed in days to come.

"I agree," he said at length.

In addition to food and ammunition, Bright Sky hoped they might also find fresh horses at Antelope Island. As he moved through the village he was conscious of the many who were on foot as a result of horses abandoned or killed along the way for one reason or another. Many of the young ones gave up their own horses in order that an old one, too exhausted to move on foot any longer, would be able to continue the journey. Even Swan had given up her prize pony. The animal now carried three small children, while she walked along beside it.

That evening, Raven brought Bright Sky word of a wounded soldier the warriors had captured. The young man had apparently been part of a rear guard detachment that had been overrun. He had been wounded and captured before his comrades were able to rescue him.

Now, wracked with pain and dying from a fatal stomach wound, he found himself surrounded by the faces of the Nez Perce warriors he'd been trying to kill but a short time ago. He sensed, somehow, the ebbing of his life force and struggled to keep it from slipping away.

Bright Sky knelt down beside him, looking down at the delicately chiseled features, which framed soft brown eyes that now reflected more pain than the young man ever imagined could be experienced.

"What is your name?" Bright Sky asked.

The eyes tried to focus while the lips formed the word "Selby."

"Which fort did you come from?" Bright Sky asked.

The young soldier coughed and sighed deeply. For a long moment Bright Sky wondered if he would respond, but presently he uttered "Fort Lewis." It meant little to Bright Sky.

"We must make the young man as comfortable as possible. It is the least we can do."

Raven nodded in agreement.

One of the young boys of the village came running up exclaiming excitedly, "They come, they come!"

"Who?"

"Two soldiers!"

Looking back toward the far end of the village, the two brothers could see two riders coming on at an easy pace, riding carefully, a large white piece of cloth tied to a pole carried by one of them. Though the distance was still too great to be sure, Bright Sky felt certain Marcus Cavanaugh was one of the riders.

Approaching the Nez Perce village, Marcus was struck by the sharp contrast between the appearance of this camp and the image of the Nez Perce village twenty years ago. Then it had been a healthy community of well-kept lodges inhabited by smiling, industrious people, generally healthy and content. Here, by comparison, were only a few ragged tipis and scruffy lean-tos. The people gathered about in clusters, looking strangely quiet and subdued. Yet at the same time, a sense of determination projected from their tired countenances.

Ahead, a figure walked slowly toward Marcus and Simon. Marcus recognized Bright Sky immediately. At twenty yards, they halted and dismounted. Simon held the reins of their mounts while Marcus stepped forward to accept the outstretched hand of his old friend. In that instant, no words were uttered and none could have equaled what was expressed in their eyes.

They sat around the small fire amid the deepening shadows of the warm autumn day. Bright Sky looked older. Marcus suspected the stress and strain of the last weeks had accelerated the process. He found himself wondering whether Bright Sky saw him in the same way.

Next to Bright Sky, Little Raven appeared lean and raptor-like, his black eyes glinting like obsidian nuggets. There was an air of aloofness, almost haughtiness, in his strong, handsome features. Marcus had forgotten what a striking individual he was.

Simon Oliver sat directly across from Little Raven, his angular torso slightly hunched over, carefully studying the Nez Perce leaders, now and then pausing in his discernment to eject a stream of tobacco juice into the small fire that danced in front of them.

"You do not give up easily, Marcus," Bright Sky said.

"Nor you, old friend," Marcus replied.

"Why do you come with the white flag?"

"To talk of the white people you are holding prisoner."

Bright Sky looked at him steadily. "We only wish them to remain with us a short time, Marcus. Then they will be set free. No harm will come to them while they are with us. You have my promise."

Marcus shook his head. "I ask you to reconsider. This was not a wise thing to do. It will only hurt your cause. And if anything happens, even an accident, you will be blamed, and the Nez Perce will suffer. What can you gain?"

Bright Sky smiled. "One thing perhaps. You will not attack us as long as they are here, out of fear that something might happen to them."

He had a point, Marcus knew it and Bright Sky knew he knew it. Reversing their roles, Marcus imagined he might well do the same thing.

"There are other soldiers in the field," Marcus said. "They may not know of the white people in your camp and attack anyway." Marcus stretched a point here. It was almost certain that the word had been spread throughout the cavalry forces.

"It matters not!" Little Raven interjected. "Each time the soldiers come we sting them!" he declared arrogantly. "Three days ago we stung them at the place of Burnt Meadows. Yesterday we stung soldiers who came at us from the north!"

Marcus looked up sharply at these last words, but said nothing.

"As always your words make sense, my old friend," Bright Sky said. "I will give it thought." The Nez Perce leader rose and extended his hand. "When next we meet let us hope the talk is of happier things."

"That is my hope as well, Bright Sky. We must both do what we can to see that it grows no worse."

Bright Sky shook his head. "Once started, such a thing is not easy to stop. It is given a life of its own and must run its course, even as we must."

"But we must never stop trying," Marcus said, accepting Bright Sky's hand. They shook with a firmness that belied their roles in the tragic pursuit.

"I think he'll turn them loose," Marcus said as he and Simon headed back to the regiment.

Both men were largely silent during the return ride, Simon, normally not being given to idle chatter to begin with, while Marcus reflected on the meeting with Bright Sky and pondered his next move.

It was late on the afternoon of the second day when they arrived back at the regiment. Marcus swung down from the saddle and after a cup of Ames' strong black coffee, directed John Brandt to bring the company commanders together.

"Better send a courier back with a report on my meeting with Bright Sky, Lieutenant. And see if we can find out who else is out here besides us. The Nez Perce mentioned contact with another force."

When the adjutant had left, Marcus eased down against a nearby tree, content to rest for a moment and savor the bitterness of Ames' strong black brew.

"We ride at first light," he explained, when the other

officers had gathered around. "By now my guess is that the Nez Perce are about here," he said, pointing to the map that was spread out before them. "It's a day and a half from here to where Simon and I met with Bright Sky. I'm sure they've moved on by now, which means they're probably two, maybe three days ahead of us. From what I understand, the logical route for them to follow is this."

He paused to trace a line on the map with a small stick, stopping at a point identified as Horsetooth Mountain.

"As I said, gentlemen, they've got the jump on us again, but we can move faster. I've seen that village. They're tired. Horsetooth Mountain is close to the border and because it's a sacred mountain, it's medicine is strong. If they can make it to Horsetooth I think they'll see the rest of the journey as a Sunday stroll."

"Any idea as to what the country is like between here and Horsetooth Mountain, Colonel?" Lieutenant Brandt asked.

"I'll let Simon answer that."

"Rough. Broken, 'specially as we get close to the Missouri," the scout explained. "Hard on men and horses, but like the colonel says, them Nez Perce is real tired, and that's got to work in our favor."

"What of the hostages, Colonel?"

"Bright Sky wants to keep them until he thinks it's safe to turn them loose. He sees them as his tribe's passport to safety. This is only a guess on my part, gentlemen, but I think he'll let them go sooner than that."

"And if he doesn't?" the irrepressible Lemaster was again playing the devil's advocate.

"Then we'll just have to work around that obstacle as best we can, Captain. An officer is supposed to be resourceful, is he not?" Marcus flashed a quick grin that suggested a confidence he wasn't really sure he felt. "That's all, gentlemen. You may see to your men."

Marcus watched them disperse, moving back through the lengthening shadows to their companies. Lemaster, as usual had posed a tantalizing question. What would they do if Bright Sky didn't release the hostages? It took no special talent to imagine the possible consequences. He could only hope it proved to be a question that never needed answering.

Chapter Thirteen

The army supply depot at Antelope Island loomed vague and indistinct in the early morning fog that swirled up out of the Missouri River. It was less an island and more a steamboat landing that had come to be called Antelope Island because it was frequented by the animals.

For some time the three Nez Perce warriors sat on their ponies in silence, studying the island, noting the occasional movement around the great piles of supplies. There appeared to be only a few soldiers. At length, satisfied, the warriors reined their mounts about and departed.

Some five miles from the island Bright Sky and Little Raven waited with the warriors for the return of the three scouts. Behind them the non-combatants moved up slowly, reflecting the fatigue of the journey. Still further back, a small party of warriors monitored their back trail, keeping a close watch on the pursuing soldiers.

Daily growing more ragged and gaunt, the number of warriors had dwindled steadily since the beginning of their odyssey. Each skirmish had exacted its pound of flesh, and though they retained the elan that distinguished their conduct thus far, the strain of the past month had begun to tell.

Bright Sky and Raven listened to the scouts' report and concluded there was little on the island to oppose them. They would seize the depot, take what supplies they needed and burn what they could not use. Thus fortified, they would be able to resume their journey.

The private lounged against the stack of packing crates, picking his teeth. He had just finished a tin of oysters, supplemented by a few stale crackers. It wasn't Delmonico's in New York, but to a hungry man this was a veritable feast. Today he was doubly fortunate in that the lieutenant had returned to the post for something or other, leaving Corporal Hubert in charge.

The lieutenant, like most lieutenants, was fussy and would have racked him up good for eating on guard duty. Corporal Hubert on the other hand was due to be discharged next month and didn't give a damn what a man did, so long as it didn't cause him any problems.

Lounging under a warm autumn sun with a belly full of oysters and crackers made the private feel comfortable and content. He wasn't taking his guard assignment seriously.

When the first yells of the Nez Perce warriors reached his ears he quickly became alert. He turned and saw a mounted Indians bearing down on him, and felt the oysters rising from the bed of his stomach.

Raising the Springfield halfway up, he bellowed for Corporal Hubert, then finished bringing the rifle to his shoulder. The index finger of his right hand was just

112

touching the trigger when a .50-caliber Spencer bullet caught him square in the middle of his forehead, killing him instantly.

Stunned at the sight of the Nez Perce warriors descending on them, seemingly from out of nowhere, the dozen soldiers and the non-commissioned officer in charge beat a hasty retreat to the far end of the island. They took refuge behind a small earthwork, hoping they would not be forced to defend the position because they had only a few weapons between them. Fortunately, the Nez Perce had eyes only for that which the troopers were there to protect in the first place.

Whooping and yelling, the warriors moved throught the stacks of supplies, some of which were stored in makeshift lean-to structures and tents. Other materiel was piled on the ground, having only recently been unloaded from the last of the season's steamboat traffic.

Foodstuffs consisted mainly of hardtack, coffee and bacon. Beyond that, the inventory ranged from standard items such as blankets, shoes, clothing, medical supplies, weapons and ammunition to the more exotic sutler's store items—tobacco, whiskey, canned oysters, peaches, and other delicacies intended to separate the bored and lonely soldier from the few dollars he earned for service.

As the excited warriors tore through pile after pile, Bright Sky and Little Raven moved among them, exhorting them to concentrate on the things they needed. Little Raven placed a guard around the whiskey to keep the livlier, more exhuberant of them from the potential danger of alcohol.

All the blankets and food were distributed to the villagers, who had finally arrived on the scene. Although relieved that there was no report of soldiers near at hand, Bright Sky was nevertheless anxious that they not spend more time there than necessary. Accordingly, as the supplies were distributed, the people forded the shallow Missouri River. Once across they would be allowed to pause and rest.

Together with her companions, Kathleen Fitzgerald watched with fascination as the Nez Perce rifled the piles of supplies, flinging things left and right. As usual, Marcy appeared to find the entire demonstration utterly compelling. In point of fact one would almost conclude that she was enjoying herself. Although Kathleen had come to grips with the reality of their situation and coped with the conditions from day to day, she found it beyond her ability to comprehend how any civilized person could be attracted to this raw, unlettered life. And yet she sensed that Marcy had somehow fallen prey to its spell.

In marked contrast, the two couples had grown increasingly morose and Kathleen had become concerned for her brother, who seemed to be the most affected of the four. If her own response had been characterized by a determination to survive, the others, Charles especially, had given up and withdrawn into themselves. Concerned though she was, however, Kathleen had decided that worry over Charles was a luxury she could ill-afford. To do so would sap the very strength she needed to survive, and she fully intended to survive.

The place was a flurry of activity as the Nez Perce scurried about, gathering anything they felt might be of use to them on their journey and transporting it across the river. Kathleen and her companions were among the first to cross the river. Once there, they were watched over by a young warrior, who would have much preferred to be with his comrades. The two Indian women who had been assigned to them were busy gathering items from the rapidly depleting depot inventory.

By late that afternoon, what remained of the depot stores were put to the torch, the flames biting into the building, tents and remaining stocks of supplies. Clouds of dense black smoke rose upward, fouling the otherwise pleasant autumn afternoon with a heavy pall and offensive odor.

Kathleen watched Bright Sky walk toward her. She was seated on a huge tree stump that had been bleached a silvery gray from many seasons of exposure to the elements. From there she had a clear view of the great burning pyre on Antelope Island.

Bright Sky studied her for a long moment before speaking. "We will leave this place soon. You and your companions will remain. There are soldiers nearby and more are following us so there is no danger for you."

She scarcely knew what to say, though the words were what she had wanted to hear from that first moment they became prisoners.

"Oh! Thank.."

He motioned her to silence. "You owe me no thanks. I, on the other hand, regret that we found it necessary for you to join us for a time. Goodbye, Miss Fitzgerald."

He turned and walked away. Kathleen whispered softly, "Goodbye and good luck to you, Bright Sky."

Marcus viewed the smoldering remains of the supply depot with a mixture of admiration and frustration, the former for Bright Sky's thoroughness, the latter for his inability to prevent what had happened. Once again, Nez Perce resourcefulness had prevailed. The supplies captured here might well give them the strength needed to reach Canada. And that was a conclusion he preferred not to contemplate.

115

He had pushed hard to cut down the distance between the regiment and the Nez Perce. The effort had paid dividends in that they were barely a day behind Bright Sky when they reached Antelope Island, only to discover that the Nez Perce had cleaned out the store and moved on.

Marcus was now also faced with the necessity of resting his horses. A few had already given out, consigning their riders to the infantry, and at the present pace, the number promised to grow.

"Twelve hours, John," he said to Lieutenant Brandt. "These animals need more than that, but right now we can't spare it."

On the brighter side, it was with great relief he discovered that the hostages had been freed. All were alive and unharmed, though reflecting the strain of their captivity. Marcus tried talking to them, thinking they might possibly have overheard something useful. However, only one of them, Kathleen Fitzgerald, proved capable of rational discussion, and she was able to provide nothing that would offer any particular insight into Bright Sky's plans. The others, although starting to come around, remained withdrawn and uncommunicative. Marcus directed that they be taken to Fort Starke under an escort provided by a platoon from A Company.

After attending to the hostages, Marcus called another council of war. The day itself had been pleasant, but now, as the arc of the sun lowered, it began to cool noticeably. A stiff breeze came at them from the northwest. The fire that Ames had built danced violently in the wind.

"Well, gentlemen, it seems we are no closer to the end of this thing than we were a month ago," Marcus declared when his officers had gathered around. "I don't know how the Nez Perce have managed to hold together. You know the shape this regiment's in. Men and horses are beat to a frazzle. Yet the Nez Perce have been able to outlast us." He paused, glancing around to see if there were comments. In each set of tired, red-rimmed eyes he saw the same thing—exhaustion.

"Bright Sky's now within reaching distance of Canada," Marcus went on. "I've had no further word from the other columns, so I'm concluding it's still up to us to catch him this side of the border."

"Begging your pardon, Colonel," Lemaster inquired with characteristic brashness. "How do we manage this miracle given the regiment's condition?"

"A not unreasonable question, Captain," Marcus answered. "I propose to take the best mounted men in the regiment and form a flying squadron. We'll travel light. Three days rations, a hundred rounds for the Springfields and thirty for the Colts. The rest of the regiment and the pack train will have to keep up as best they are able."

Following the conference, Marcus remained in front of the fire, warming himself. Ames interrupted with a fresh cup of coffee, then disappeared into the darkness.

"Let me sweeten that for you a bit, Marcus," Simon Oliver offered, stepping out of the shadows into the firelight.

"Bright Sky was thorough, but not totally complete," the scout said with a grin, adding a portion of whisky to Marcus' cup. "Helps to cut the chill."

Marcus felt the warmth of the hot, black, whisky-laced coffee course through his system. "I couldn't have picked a better time and place for that than here tonight."

"I figured that," Simon agreed. "Another?"

Marcus shook his head. "We'll down a whole bottle

when this thing's over, Simon, but for now I need a clear head. Any thoughts?"

The scout let a long moment pass before responding. "Yeah," he said finally and with a surprising softness in his voice. "Let 'em go, Marcus."

Sensing that his suggestion had caught Marcus by surprise, Simon added, "What'll it hurt, Marcus? They're not renegades like Sitting Bull and Crazy Horse. These Nez Perce don't want anything but to get away. I say let 'em go."

Marcus shook his head. "I wish it was that easy, Simon, but there's too much involved here. This thing reaches all the way up to Congress and the White House now. No, it's too late for that, my friend. Too big. National prestige is on the line."

The scout finished his coffee. "For Bright Sky's sake, if he's gonna get caught I hope it's by us, Marcus. Liable to be tougher on the Nez Perce if one of them other columns gets there first."

"I've thought of that, too," Marcus said, thinking especially of Maynard "Mad" Norris. "And I don't intend to let that happen."

"You may not have any choice," Simon said. "We've no idea where Norris or anyone else is."

"I realize that, Simon. Let's just say I've got a hunch we're closer to the Nez Perce than anyone else, at least for the moment."

"Well, you ain't too bad with your hunches as I recall, but we'll see how you do with this one. See you in the saddle, Marcus," Simon Oliver said. He rose to his feet and disappeared into the darkness.

The fire dwindled. Marcus added a handful of small branches that Ames had conveniently gathered, and watched the flames bite into the fresh fuel. Suddenly he felt very tired. Stretching out, he lay back against his

118

saddle and covered himself with the single blanket. He noted the clarity of the night sky and thought he might find frost in the morning. He did not remember Ames covering him with a second blanket.

Chapter Fourteen

They would never have gotten as close to the Nez Perce camp as they did had it not been for a violent thunderstorm that pounded the region. Anson Demarest and his volunteers drove their horses mercilessly through the drenching downpour, a column of ghostly riders silhouetted against a foreboding landscape by flashing bursts of menacing lightning. Hunched over their saddles, sunk down into their slickers, and mostly hungover from the prodigious quantities of whiskey consumed the night before, they pushed on along a course that would eventually cut the Nez Perce trail.

Still smarting from his rebuke at the hands of the military in general and Colonel Marcus Cavanaugh in particular, Anson Demarest vowed they would deal with the Nez Perce thieves and murderers in their own way. If the army was unwilling or unable to get the job done, then he would.

Following their dismissal by Cavanaugh, the so-called Ramsey Rangers had started back to Ramsey. Enroute, Demarest had suggested that a council of war was appropriate. With no dissenters, they had uncorked a few bottles and proceeded to discuss Indian-hunting strategy, Ramsey Ranger style.

As the discussion progressed, one dominant question emerged. What was to stop them from launching their own campaign? Such business promised a lot more in the way of excitement than they were ever likely to experience by working with the army. Not surprisingly, the discussion resulted in vows to resolve the Nez Perce problem once and for all. To hell with Colonel Marcus Cavanaugh. To hell with the Army.

Their strategy was simple. Ramsey was situated roughly halfway between Fort Casey and Horsetooth Mountain. The country in that immediate area was well known to most of them. Instead of continuing north to Ramsey, they decided to angle off to the east and cut the trail of the Nez Perce well ahead of the army. Then they'd give those red whelps a taste of real soldierin'.

Reinforced by the power of old forty-rod, the volunteers set forth on their frontier crusade. At their head rode Anson Demarest, a sardonic smile etched on his unshaven visage. For the volunteers, it was the benevolence of a sympathetic God that gave them, first, the cover of the storm to screen their approach, and second, the good fortune to bumble across the Nez Perce trail and move within striking distance of the Indian camp.

The storm rumbled off into the eastern distance, giving way to the vigor of a glorious autumn day, chill and brisk, but scrubbed, rinsed and ready to serve. Had they been properly organized and disciplined, the volunteers might indeed have been able to accomplish what the army had not quite been unable to. However, as someone observed, the hound could have caught the hare had it not paused to lift its leg.

While Anson Demarest and a companion reconnoitered the Nez Perce position, a disagreement developed between two of the rangers as to what they ought to be doing.

"I say we ought to ride right in there. Hit 'em straight on," a man known as Brush argued.

Brush's most vocal opponent, an older man named Wes, shook his head. "I say wait 'til Anse gets back. We ought to know what the place looks like 'fore we do anything."

Some around him nodded in agreement, seeing the sense of his logic.

"I'm tired of ridin' and waitin'," Brush declared, taking a long pull of his nearly empty whiskey bottle.

"If you was to back off that bottle for a while it might clear up your head," Wes said.

"I'll back off when I'm damn good and ready. What's more it strikes me maybe you're a little yellow, Wes. I got a feelin' you're afraid of them Nez Perce. Maybe that's why you'd rather wait."

Brush said it low and accusingly, knowing full well that he had given Wes no choice but to act. The older man wasted no time, surprising Brush with the swiftness of his movement.

His reflexes dulled by the whiskey, Brush was unable to avoid the big fist that caught him flush in the face, smashing his nose and splattering blood across his front. He tried to turn away and find a position from which to defend himself, but Wes gave him no quarter. Brush struck out wildly with a flaying fist and felt it strike some part of Wes's face. Then, as the latter's big meaty hands closed around his throat, he struggled and twisted, fighting for air.

122

With one free hand he found his Colt and pulled it from its holster. Bringing the weapon up, he jabbed it in Wes's mid-section and pulled the trigger. The boom of the big revolver echoed through the early morning. Wes went limp and fell to the ground. Brush struggled to his feet, gagging as he sucked in lungfulls of air. Around them, the rest of the Ramsey Rangers looked on, sober, quiet and unemotional.

Something like a quarter of a mile away, Anson Demarest, peering over a low ridge heard the boom of the big Colt and swore softly. Beyond the ridge, the same shot reached the ears of the Nez Perce. In this case, to be forewarned meant forearmed.

Brush gave the order to charge the Indian encampment. Like the rowdy mob they were, the Ramsey Rangers charged across the four-hundred-yard stretch of ground between their assembly point at the base of the low ridge and the Nez Perce, shouting and whooping. The Rangers never expected the kind of resistance that was hurled at them, Indian bullets emptying many saddles before their riders even reached the camp.

Stunned, a few of the Rangers reined up and milled about, uncertain as to what exactly they ought to do. Their hesitancy proved contagious, dissolving the attack and forcing the volunteers to search for any protection they could find. From behind hillocks, shallow depressions and an occasional scrub tree the volunteers returned the Indians' fire.

With Little Raven leading, the Nez Perce closed in on the disorganized volunteers, many of whom were firing wildly and represented more danger to their comrades than they did the Nez Perce.

From the low finger of a ridge to the north, one group of Nez Perce poured fire down on one flank of the volunteer position. Meanwhile, along the front, warriors moved in, slowly, methodically, adding the pressure of their fire to that hitting the defenders from the flank.

Anson Demarest had one of the least exposed positions, behind a mound of boulders at the edge of a shallow depression. They were barely large enough to accommodate his substantial form. Long considered an opportunist by himself as well as those who knew him, when the charge stalled Demarest quickly recognized the situation and wasted no time seeking the best place to be.

From there he carefully selected targets of opportunity for his old Sharps buffalo rifle, which he was able to use with considerable accuracy. He managed to dispatch, by his own count, four Nez Perce warriors. On each occasion, he smiled and thought of General Phil Sheridan's dictum that the best Indians were dead ones. A philosophy that Anson Demarest fully embraced, it was about to prove his undoing.

Consumed as he was by this passion for destruction, Demarest now acted out of character. The long ridge to his left offered a number of targets, but he was especially attracted to one Indian who seemed a commanding presence. He fairly drooled at the thought of lining that son-of-a-red-mother up in his sights. The angle from his position, however, was not a favorable one, and the distance was great, even for a rifleman of Demarest's ability. That, however, was not going to prevent him from trying.

He eased his bulk out of the small depression. Crouching, then waddling, now crawling, he moved through the other volunteers, drawing fire that was occasionally close, until he reached a small hummock about midway between his old position and the ridge.

He adjusted his position, leveled out the Sharps and

waited. When the trophy again presented itself, Demarest lined-up the sights on his rifle, held steady and squeezed. The big gun bucked backward as it launched its missle across the two hundred yards separating the two men. For a moment, Demarest, thinking he might have missed, was about to curse. But the Indian buckled and dropped. The Sharps—'Old Comfort" he had dubbed his gun—had done its job again.

As a reward, Anson Demarest paused in his labors long enough to slice off a chaw of burley, which he deposited in his mouth, and started back to the security of his old spot. He likely would have made it too, had not one of the volunteers hollered out for old lard-ass to move out of the way. Angered at the charge, Demarest rose to the occasion just in time to greet a forty-four caliber Winchester slug that was not intended for him, but which found him a convenient stopping place anyway. He felt the soapy smack of the bullet in the same instant that he greeted eternity.

Little Raven knew nothing about the men who were attacking except that they were not soldiers.

Sliding obliquely along the crest of the ridge where a dozen warriors were returning the fire of the attackers, Raven shouted words of encouragement, reminding them that their supply of ammunition was limited. Twice he was warned to keep down, but as always, he spurned the safe course, believing a warrior leader must set an example by publicly scorning fear. Thus it was that when he rose too far on the third occasion a bullet pierced his heart perfectly. Little Raven died instantly.

When the battle was over, and the civilian volunteers had fled, the braves brought Little Raven's body to Bright Sky. Gently they laid the body of the young warrior leader at his brother's feet. Tears welled up in Bright Sky's eyes.

"How did it happen?" he demanded angrily.

"He was on the ridge, guiding us, always urging us to have courage. We were afraid such a thing might happen, but he called us women and said his medicine was strong."

For a long moment, Bright Sky was engulfed by a sense of loss that overpowered his mind. He was catapulted back to when he and Raven were boys again, learning to hunt and ride in those long summers before the Nez Perce were forced onto the reservation.

"I don't think those were soldiers," a warrior was explaining. "See this one that we have captured. He is not dressed as the soldiers dress and does not act like them."

Bright Sky walked over to where a captive sat on the ground, guarded by two warriors. The man looked dirty and arrogant. It was clear that the man was no soldier. That puzzled and worried Bright Sky. Where had he come from? Apparently the Indians had more to concern themselves with than soldiers.

Suddenly he had the thought that this was the man who had killed Raven and he was forced to curtail an overpowering desire to take his life in exchange. The intention must have been evident on his face because the man's face turned white with fear.

"Bind him and leave him here when we go," he said at length, "There is nothing he can do for us now."

He felt a hand on his arm and recognized the touch.

"I am sorry," Swan said softly.

He turned to look at her and saw in her eyes a strength that he longed to possess. She was always there. It seemed he could scarcely recall a time when she was not. If Little Raven had been his right arm,

Swan had been his left. And now he truly felt like a man that had lost an arm.

"I wonder why we continue," he said at length, sighing.

"Because of the people. All of us," she replied simply. "Many have been left behind that others might find the peace and freedom we all seek."

Bright Sky smiled at her. "You should have been chief."

She shook her head. "I have not the wisdom, but you do, my husband."

"I wish I felt that certain." He stared into the northern distance where gray skies looked ominous.

"You must not think so much about it. Let your thoughts instead be on today and what we are to do next. The wisdom will take care of itself."

He nodded. She was right. Wisdom would come from the many things small and large that made up each day. It was time to turn his thoughts back to those things that needed immediate attention. To fail in this would be to say that Raven and all of the others had died for nothing. He closed his eyes and breathed a prayer that he be granted strength to see that those who had suffered had done so in order that the rest might reach the Land of the Grandmother.

The Indians struck north early the next morning. It was cold and somber. There was ice on the surface of the nearby creek and steam issued from the mouths and nostrils of people and animals alike.

Bright Sky walked with Stone Bear, on whom he would depend for warrior council now that Raven was gone. Bear was a fine warrior, too. Somewhat older than Raven and larger physically, Bear was solid and dependable if not quite as resourceful and imaginative as Little Raven.

"I will try and serve you as well as Little Raven," Bear said after they had walked in silence for a time.

Stopping, Bright Sky turned to look into the eyes of the big warrior, placing a hand on his shoulder. "We are fortunate to have a warrior such as you to guard us."

Bear rose to his full height and smiled proudly. "The people are fortunate to have a leader like you. And now I must join my warriors." He grasped Bright Sky's upper arm firmly, swung onto his pony and galloped back through the exodus of marching people.

There had been no sign of soldiers for several days. Perhaps the Indians had at last outdistanced Marcus Cavanaugh and any others who were after them. But the Grandmother Land was still three days journey away, Bright Sky thought, and it would be important to remain alert until his people were safely across the border.

Michael Bright Sky became conscious of a small form trudging alongside him and looked down at a small boy, half running, half walking in an effort to maintain pace with him. The boy was perhaps ten and willowy, more so than normal because of what he'd gone through of late.

"You walk like a warrior. What are you called?" Bright Sky asked.

The lad looked up at him and grinned, pleased that his great leader had seen fit to call him a warrior.

"Little Wolf," the lad answered.

Bright Sky nodded. "Your father was Big Wolf, the one who died so bravely at the Firehole."

The boy nodded. "Yes. He was a fine warrior."

"We owe him a great deal," Bright Sky said. "We owe all those who have given their lives that we might continue our journey. Yes, your father was a fine warrior," he said, placing a hand on the youth's shoulder. "And I know you, too, will be a fine warrior, one the people can look to, just as they looked to your father."

"I am ready now," the boy said, eagerly.

Bright Sky smiled. "I know. One thing a warrior must learn is patience. You must learn to wait and watch for the right moment. When the time comes, I will call, but for now you must help those who struggle. And now I must ride ahead."

Little Wolf nodded. "I will do as you say."

Bright Sky swung onto his horse and put the animal into a lope toward the head of the caravan.

Chapter Fifteen

They rode hard, one hundred and eighteen men in three under-strength companies. Gaunt and beaten down from the rigors of campaigning, they resembled more a motley collection of prairie rats than a flying squadron of United States Cavalry.

The concept was not new. Marcus had seen it used in both Arizona and Dakota against the Apache and Sioux. It involved stripping down a column of troops of the fittest men and horses to the bare essentials, and sending them on ahead to hold the enemy until the main body could be brought up.

Since leaving Antelope Island two days ago, Marcus had pushed his flying squadron to the limit, halting only long enough to provide a brief rest for men and animals. The country was broken just as Simon had promised, a land of buttes and hummocks, cut by numerous arroyos. Above, the sky was pale blue, filled with thick, scudding clouds of somber gray.

Yesterday they had come upon the battered remnants of the Ramsey Rangers, heading back to their home base, tired, beaten and humiliated. Marcus had little sympathy for what he considered a vigilante mob. They had damn well gotten what they deserved. When they asked for an escort, he refused and ordered the flying squadron to resume its pursuit.

"I figure they're a day ahead at the most," Simon reported, reining his mount in alongside Marcus. "Temperature's dropping, Marcus. And these old bones tell me we kin figure to see some snow real soon."

Marcus glanced at the flint-gray sky and nodded. "My bones are too tired to tell me anything about the weather, Simon."

The scout chuckled and gestured back toward the column. "You've had these boys in the saddle so much they won't ever want to set again, Marcus. I been hearin' some real uncomplimentary things 'bout you here of late."

Marcus grinned. "I'd be surprised and worried if it was otherwise."

Ahead of them, ridges and buttes dominated the distant skyline that stretched to Canada, stark and ominous beneath a threatening sky. Underfoot, close-cropped buffalo grass interspersed with tall stands of purple lupine waved in the chilly breeze.

Marcus called an hour halt in a low valley cut by a small creek. The troopers were permitted to build small coffee fires, unsaddle and issue the horses a ration of oats from the dwindling supply. Marcus shared coffee with Brandt, Lemaster and Simon Oliver.

"Have your point men alerted," Marcus said to Lemaster. "Simon says they're not far ahead so we can expect something almost anytime. What I don't want is more surprises."

"Be hard to say who's liable to be more surprised,

them or us," Stephen Lemaster said, his voice edgy with fatigue.

For a long moment the silence deepened. "We're all tired, Stephen," Marcus responded in a soft, controlled voice. He addressed the captain by his first name, a familiarity he seldom took with his officers, John Brandt excepted. "But I trust you can stay awake for another few hours anyway."

As one recognized for his appreciation of sleep, Marcus' remark eased the tension and brought a smile even to Lemaster's unshaven face.

"Thanks for the coffee, Colonel." Pulling the collar of his buckskin jacket up around his neck, Lemaster headed back to his company.

Simon Oliver looked at Marcus, shrugged and walked over to saddle his horse. Brandt dumped the dregs of his coffee into the ashes of the fire.

"Let's move out, gentlemen," Marcus said.

As usual, Simon Oliver's estimate was not far off the mark. About mid-afternoon, the point party found the Nez Perce rear guard. When the staccato sounds of their clash reached him, Marcus immediately spurred the column forward.

The Nez Perce rear guard was positioned along a ridgeline that extended half a mile to the south. Halting, Marcus threw out a platoon of skirmishers, then directed Lemaster to sweep around to the south and come up behind the rear guard.

The Nez Perce, however, proved elusive. They fell back to a new position just in time to avoid being flanked. Through the remainder of the afternoon the process repeated itself, with the Nez Perce always managing to extricate themselves at the last moment. As darkness closed in, it was accompanied by light flakes of snow that swirled through the air, at first melting as they struck the ground, then sticking as the evening deepened.

The tactic of the rear guard was working, buying time for the Nez Perce, but the worriors couldn't continue it indefinitely. Neither could Cavanaugh's men for that matter. If Bright Sky was to be stopped short of the border, it was going to take more help than the colonel had available. True, the rest of the regiment was coming up, but in its ragged condition, it was almost more of a liability than an asset.

"I've got a bit of a shelter rigged up, Colonel," Ames said, interrupting his thoughts.

"What? Oh, yes. Thanks, Ames."

Marcus huddled under the meager lean-to, savoring the tin of steaming coffee, wishing Simon would come over and offer to sweeten it with something that would take a man's mind off the infernal weather. Seemed like it was either too hot or too cold whenever he was in the field.

"You want the last of this, Colonel?" Simon Oliver inquired, poking his head under the lean-to, wiping the heavy, wet snow from his face. His bony hand clutched a near empty flask.

"As a matter of fact, Simon . . . " Marcus responded, holding his coffee tin out.

The two men sipped their coffee-plus in silence. Presently, they were joined by Lieutenant Brandt and the three company commanders.

"We don't have the strength to exploit contact like we had today, so all we can do is keep after them," Marcus said. Picking up a small stick, he traced their position in the snow. "Here we are right about so." He marked an X in the snow. "And here's Horsetooth Mountain, two days from here." He drew a square to indicate the mountain. "If they get beyond Horsetooth we'll have almost no chance of stopping them. So to repeat myself, we keep after them. Tomorrow. The next day. With no rest."

"For them or us," Brandt observed.

"That's right," Marcus observed. "Creighton, your company will make up the point in the morning. We'll change that as often as possible. Just keep in mind that the idea is to maintain the pressure on the Nez Perce."

"What about other columns in the field, Colonel?"

"No idea at the moment," Marcus answered. "Though I believe Colonel Norris may be closer than we know. The latest word we had was that Norris would be the third force, moving north from Fort Starke. Colonel Taylor was the other column, but we don't know whether he is still in the field or not."

The huge flakes of soft, wet snow suggested a pastoral setting, one that conflicted and contrasted somehow with men making plans to wage war. At the conclusion of the conference, Marcus asked Simon to stay.

"I can smell something comin' my way, Marcus."

Marcus nodded. "You always did have a good nose, my friend."

"What's on your mind, Marcus?"

"Not much," Marcus replied after a moment. "Want you to take a little ride, Simon."

"To where?"

"Find Maynard Norris for me."

"Yeah, I allow maybe that's a little ride and then some," Simon observed. "You got any idea where he might be?"

Marcus unrolled his well worn field map, pointed at Fort Starke and ran his finger in a general northwesterly direction toward Horsetooth Mountain. He pursed his lips and frowned thoughtfully.

"Well, in that last communique we had from him,

Abrams indicated Norris would take the field in two days, and that's a week ago. So assuming that happened and allowing for the usual progress of an army column in the field, I'd say that ought to put Maynard Norris right about here." Marcus paused to jab his finger at a point on the map about thirty miles south of Horsetooth Mountain.

"Two days ride southwest more or less," Simon observed. "Leave in the morning?"

"How about now, Simon?"

The scout pushed his hat back and took a deep breath. "You're a hard man, Colonel, but under the circumstances I allow it's the thing to do. You mind if I finish my coffee?

Marcus grinned. "Finish your coffee, Simon. Then find Maynard Norris for me."

Snow swirled about, and the heavy white wetness began to accumulate as Simon Oliver finished his last cup of strong black coffee. Then he swung onto his Morgan gelding and headed south into the night. Simon was unaware of the man watching him disappear behind the curtain of snowflakes.

"Ride carefully, Simon," Marcus said, half aloud.

Hat pulled down and all but engulfed by his slicker, Simon Oliver rode steadily, his eyes peering out from beneath the battered, gray felt hat. As the eastern sky gradually began to lighten, the storm intensified. Where the flakes had been soft and gentle, they were now smaller and icy. From long experience in these situations, Simon Oliver sensed that he was about to be caught in an early season blizzard. He had to find himself a spot to hole up until it was over.

Luck was with him. A hundred yards later he discovered a small sheltered draw. Dismounting, he quickly unsaddled and tethered the horse, his hands already almost too numb to feel. Wet clothes, he knew, would lose no time freezing to his body. He'd seen these storms before, been part of them and knew what had to be done—and quickly.

A young cottonwood nearby provided a couple of limbs that served as uprights for a lean-to that he covered with boughs. Then, gathering an armload of dry branches, he managed to start a small fire at the opening of his make-shift shelter. As it gained strength, he added larger pieces, taking comfort from the heat that was reflected back into the hastily-made shelter.

From his saddlebags he produced a small flask. He held it up and spoke aloud. "Sorry, Marcus, but I always save one for emergencies, and I figure this here's a bonafide emergency."

Having thus toasted the man who had ordered him on this journey, Simon Oliver drank long and felt much the better for it. Pulling out a small can, he filled it with snow and placed it on the fire to melt, a process he repeated until there was enough water for coffee. When the water had boiled, he made the coffee, adding the last of the whiskey. He hurled the empty flask out into the storm.

From his bags he also produced a pouch of dried buffalo meat, part of which he consumed. After adding more fuel to the small fire, he pulled his hat down and drew the single blanket around him to wait out the storm.

As near as he could tell, it was noon the next day when the storm showed signs of easing up. Stiff and hungry, Simon roused himself, took care of his bodily needs, then saddled the gelding and resumed his journey. By late afternoon a clearing sky greeted him, and that evening the sun set in a crimson wash across the western horizon.

He camped that night under a cold but crystal-clear sky so bright with countless star patterns it fairly hurt a man's eyes to look at it. He had chosen his spot carefully, for this was still country in which a man could find Sioux and Cheyenne that were apt to be less than hospitable. True, most of the hostiles had gone off to Canada, but not all, and one did well to bear such things in mind.

The next day found him riding south through what promised to be another spell of golden autumn weather. A warming sun made quick work of the wet snow and by noon the temperature had warmed noticeably.

It was pushing late afternoon when he noted the smoke rising in the distance and shortly recognized the white tents for what they were—an army bivouac. Marcus Cavanaugh had more or less been right about the whereabouts of Colonel Norris.

Approaching the camp, he was challenged by a sentry. After identifying himself to the corporal of the guard, he was taken to see Norris, a man Simon had heard much of, but had never met.

He found "Mad" Maynard Norris seated behind a small writing desk in his tent. A striking figure, Norris was tall and powerfully built, with dark brown hair that was starting to thin slightly and a full mustache. He appeared to be in his forties, just beginning to show evidence of an expanding waistline. Simon guessed he knew how to enjoy a meal.

The scout also found Maynard Norris an attentive listener as information about the Nez Perce situation was presented to him. He asked pointed questions designed to get to the heart of the matter.

With his staff gathered around, Norris bent over a large map of the territory, studying it intently while Simon filled him in on details, pointing out Cavanaugh's last position and the direction the Nez Perce were marching in.

"Horsetooth Mountain. That's the spot," Norris observed.

Simon nodded. "That's the way me and Marcus see it, too."

"Colonel Cavanaugh, a good man," Norris said, continuing his survey of the map.

"You'll get no argument from me, Colonel," Simon agreed.

Norris straightened up and looked at the scout, flashing a quick smile. "Yes, I'd have been surprised had you offered one," he said. "My command will march at dawn, Mr. Oliver. You of course are free to join my cadre of scouts, though I rather expect you'd prefer to rejoin Colonel Cavanaugh."

Simon nodded. "I'll leave at first light."

"Very well," Norris said. "Now as to a working plan. My adjutant will prepare something official, but I'll give you an oral version to make certain there's an understanding as to what's afoot here." Norris paused to look at the map again before continuing.

"My scouts tell me there's a spot about half a mile from Horsetooth with good cover. We can be there in two days, which is about how long it will take you to get back. Now, if I have this clear in my mind, Colonel Cavanaugh is about two days from the mountain."

Norris paused again to look at Simon for confirmation. "So, you may advise Colonel Cavanaugh that unless circumstances dictate otherwise, we will meet on the twenty-second and attack the Nez Perce at dawn on the Twenty-fourth."

138

"Yes sir, I'll pass that on." Simon saw the hunger in the man's eyes and realized then that this was a man who never supported anyone without a good reason. The scout concluded that everything he'd heard about Norris was probably true.

Simon had breakfast with Norris' scouts at dawn, wolfing down bacon, hard bread and strong black coffee. He knew some of those seated around the fire and was glad for the chance to renew old acquaintances. He left quickly. As the gelding picked its way north beneath a brightening sky, he had the distinct feeling the end of the chase was close at hand.

Chapter Sixteen

Brigadier General Carlton Milhew Abrams stood at the window of his second story office, looking out at the steady drizzle which was now in its second day. Tall and spare, with iron-gray hair and beard, he was a dignified man, and proud of the empty left sleeve pinned to his coat. It was a legacy from the Civil War battle of Peachtree Creek during the Atlanta Campaign.

With practiced ease the general twirled the cigar slowly around in his mouth, pondering the dilemma that confronted and confounded him. The damned Nez Perce had been on the run for a month now, and giving everyone the fits in the process. He had virtually stripped all of the garrisons in his department to round them up, but the blasted Indians had managed to elude or make fools of them all.

"Damn it, Abe," a gruff voice behind him said. "Haven't you got someone in your department who can catch and hang on to those people?"

Abrams sighed and threw up his hands. "Hell,

Cump . . . " he began, addressing the General of the Army by a sobriquet reserved for family and close friends. The two had served together throughout the war and that experience had forged a firm bond between them. In one-on-one situations such as this they spoke to each other as friends, rather than commander and subordinate. "You were damn lucky to get out of Yellowstone when you did or they would nabbed you as a hostage, too."

Red-bearded, tousled-headed General William Tecumseh Sherman expelled a cloud of blue cigar smoke and grunted. "Suppose I was at that," he admitted. "But by thunder, Abe, those people have got to be stopped! Surely, if we could stop Bedford Forrest we can catch a few Indians."

Carlton Abrams smiled. "I wasn't aware you caught Forrest. Appomattox just made it a convenient stopping point."

Sherman grunted again. "And what about those volunteers? The story I got was that they wound up getting shot to pieces, and that the army refused to cooperate with them."

"Cump, you know these volunteers."

Sherman nodded and took a deep drag of his cigar. "I knew thousands in the war. So did you, Abe. Damn fine bunch. We'd not have licked the Rebs without them."

"Agreed, Cump, but these are a different breed. Vigilantes is all they are. Looking for a legal way to kill Indians is what they're after."

"Well, no matter. We've got to end this fast. Abe, do you have any idea how much pressure President Arthur is feeling over this thing?"

Abrams frowned and drew on his cigar. "Plenty, I suppose."

Sherman stood up and extended his hand. "Do whatever you have to, Abe. I'll back you up. You'll have help. Maynard Norris is in the field and Taylor is or will be shortly. Let's end it quickly and quietly, Abe."

Abrams accepted the outstretched hand and gripped it firmly. "See you in Washington next spring, Cump."

When Sherman had gone, Abrams paced back and forth, rolling the cigar between his fingers as was his habit when in deep thought. He wondered where Colonel Cavanaugh was at that precise moment. He had first known Marcus as a fresh young lieutenant during the war. Abrams had been impressed by the young man's soldierly qualities then, and had never had reason to revise his opinion.

He was certain Cavanaugh was doing all he could to conclude the Nez Perce problem, but sometimes circumstances simply exceeded anyone's ability to control them. Unfortunately, that seldom mitigated the impact of accountability for whoever happened to be in charge. He hoped Marcus Cavanaugh would not have to bear the brunt of that justice.

He walked to the door and summoned his adjutant, a balding, bespectacled captain who entered the room and came immediately to attention.

"At ease, Captain. Send a message to Colonel Cavanaugh." Abrams paused, then waved the captain off. "On second thought, don't bother."

"Sir?"

"Never mind, Captain. Colonel Cavanaugh's beyond the reach of the telegraph right now. It will have to wait until he gets back to Fort Casey."

"Yes, sir," the captain saluted, wheeled about and left.

Abrams hated not being in the field himself. At department headquarters he was in a vacuum. Nothing happened there except paperwork. He felt like a prisoner. Sherman had given him an ultimatum, yet there was not a blasted thing he could do other than wait and hope people like Marcus Cavanaugh got the job done. He knew well what the troops would be enduring in the field, but would have given anything to exchange their difficulties for his own. Sometimes, as he did now, Carlton Abrams felt the price of promotion and advancement in the army was not satisfaction but frustration.

The storm that caught Simon Oliver temporarily halted Marcus' pursuit. With supplies and ammunition running low, he elected to rest for an additional twenty-four hours after the weather cleared to give the remaining companies of the regiment and the pack train time to join them.

Assessing the regiment's current capability was a discouraging proposition. Of the eight original companies he'd begun the campaign with, the better part of three were without serviceable horses at present and the rate was rising. Ammunition was also beginning to run low. They'd figured to replenish their stock at Antelope Island, but the Nez Perce raid had eliminated that possibility.

Given the circumstances, Marcus reshuffled his command again. The dismounted men from each company were organized into two temporary companies of infantry and assigned to the pack train. The remaining five companies were organized into two battalions. The first, commanded by Lemaster, consisted of Companies A, B and F, while Pat Foster's second battalion had G and H Companies.

Thirty-six hours after the storm passed, Simon Oliver splashed his gelding across the Milkweed River and rode into camp.

"You find Norris?" Marcus asked.

Simon nodded. "For the price of a cup of coffee I'll tell you all about it."

Glancing about, Simon couldn't help but note the difference in the appearance of Marcus' command compared to Maynard Norris'. The Eleventh Cavalry had been on almost continuous field duty for a month, while Norris' much heralded foot soldiers looked trim and proper.

"Your boys wouldn't pass muster in Norris' camp," Simon observed with a wry grin.

"These boys will stand and fight with anybody at any time," Marcus vowed.

"My sentiments exactly," the scout agreed.

Finding a relatively dry spot, Marcus spread out his field map on the ground and watched as Simon pointed to key locations as he summarized his discussion with Norris.

"The Nez Perce must be close to Horsetooth, if not there by now," the scout said.

"And from there it can't be much more than thirty miles to the border," Marcus added. "And Norris suggests a conference on the Twenty-second?"

Simon nodded.

"Well, we'd better get started," Marcus said, half aloud, continuing his study of the map. "Bright Sky hasn't been pressured by us the past forty-eight hours and I'm inclined to think he just might be feeling a little safer than he really is."

"Makes sense," Simon agreed.

The sky began to darken as the day wore on.

"And if there's more bad weather moving in he just might be moved to stay put at Horsetooth for an extra day or two to rest his people."

"Course you know what's gonna happen if Bright

Sky decides not to hang around, Marcus. It'll be your ass."

Marcus nodded. "Maybe, but it goes with the job, Simon."

"Well, the rest of the regiment's up now. You could push ahead and close the door on Bright Sky without takin' any chances. You and the Eleventh would get the credit, which is the way it oughta be. But consider this, Marcus. If Maynard Norris plays a part in this you know who's gonna' claim it."

Marcus nodded, a mock smile crossing his face. "Simon, are you questioning the integrity of an army officer?"

The scout held up his hands in mock horror. "Never let it be said."

Marcus chuckled, then grew serious again. "I appreciate your concern, Simon, and I admit there's a risk involved here. Bright Sky could decide to press on and leave all of us looking like a bunch of fools, which he's managed to do pretty well anyway. But there's also a risk involved if we move in without support. We haven't the manpower to contain the Nez Perce without Norris' men. So that leaves us with a rendezvous to keep, friend Simon."

Marcus directed Brandt to sound officers call. Ten minutes later the officers gathered to listen to their newest set of instructions.

"Simon and I will take a small escort and locate Colonel Norris. Captain Lemaster, you will command the regiment in my absence. Your orders are to bring the two mounted battalions to an assembly area here along the lower Milkweed River," Marcus said, pointing on the map to an area south of Horsetooth Mountain. "There should be no trouble concealing the regiment from the Nez Perce camp. I'll rejoin you at that point.

The pack train and dismounted men will follow as closely as possible. If things go as expected I expect to finish this campaign soon."

Despite the threat of another storm moving in, Marcus and Simon, together with a sergeant and five enlisted men, struck out in the darkening afternoon, pushing on through the twilight into full darkness before Marcus called a halt for the night.

Not wanting to take a chance on calling attention to his groups, Marcus allowed no fires, which made for a long, cold night, punished by a howling wind that pierced everything with its knife-like edge. The men welcomed the arrival of dawn and the resumption of movement.

Horsetooth Mountain was easily identifiable, even from a distance. They found Norris in camp late the next afternoon, just as he had promised to be, having arrived earlier that day with a small escort.

"Well, Mr. Oliver, I did not expect to see you again so soon. And this of course is Colonel Marcus Cavanaugh. Honored, sir!" Norris extended his hand.

"It is a great honor for me, Colonel Norris. Your record is well known."

"As is yours, Colonel Cavanaugh, but come, such things are better discussed over food."

"I appreciate the offer to share your table, Colonel, but I'm afraid any discussion of our respective reputations will have to wait for another time. Right now I think we need to finalize our strategy."

Maynard Norris looked at him squarely for a long moment, then smiled. "Of course, Colonel. First things first, eh?"

Norris spread his maps across the small table. Flickering candles on either side cast fingers of shadows across the map. Pointing with the tip of an unusually long, slender index finger, Norris reviewed again the strategy he'd discussed with Simon.

"I like your idea of coming in from the south and sending a force around to cut off any escape to Canada. Good plan, Colonel Cavanaugh. My command can be in position for a dawn attack the day after tomorrow on the 24th if that is acceptable to you."

"Yes, we should be able to manage that," Marcus said.

"Very well then. Why don't I open the show with my howitzer. That will be your cue to attack, Colonel. I will come in from the east and also send a detachment around to the north to cut off any escape. That should fit perfectly with your plan." He paused momentarily, tugging gently on his mustache. "Oh by the way, you did know that my commission antedates your own, did you not?"

Out of the corner of his own eye, Marcus glimpsed Simon rolling his eyes. "No, I did not know that, Colonel. Well, then, as senior officer here, you are of course in tactical command."

Their eyes met and locked for a long instant. Marcus sensed the flint hardness in the legendary figure that stood across from him. Theatrics aside, Maynard Norris was capable of being as ruthless as he needed to be, Marcus decided. Suddenly Norris flashed the smile for which he was so famous.

"A formality, Colonel Cavanaugh. We're in this together. We've a job to do and that's what we must see to." Norris extended his hand again, which Marcus accepted.

"Norris has got three reporters with him," Simon said, as he and Marcus rode back to the regiment. "And you can bet your last chaw that the story the public reads will be how Maynard Norris whipped the Nez

Perce with the help of Marcus Cavanaugh. I can see the headlines now."

"Maybe, Simon. Maybe. But I don't care. What matters to me is that the most lives as possible can be spared—on both sides."

Chapter Seventeen

Bold tongues of yellow and orange flame taunted the gathering darkness that brought with it a wind of chill. On this night, however, knowing that the wind had honed its edge in the Grandmother Country tempered Michael Bright Sky's feeling for its cutting cold.

As he walked through the camp the Nez Perce chief felt a sense of urgency. The people were much in need, and it pained him that as their leader he was unable to help. He felt a tug on the blanket that he'd wrapped around his shoulders, looked down and saw Little Wolf.

"I am ready," the boy said.

"And so you are," Bright Sky agreed, turning to look down at the boy, hands on his hips.

"You have only to ask and I will take care of it," the boy said proudly and with conviction.

Bright Sky nodded, smiling. "With such as you, no leader would ever have trouble," he told the boy, who beamed with pride.

"But what would you have me do?" he asked, the expression on his face matching his grave tone of voice.

Bright Sky grew serious as he addressed the boy's concern. "Well, let me see. Aaah, yes, I have it! We need a good warrior to watch the horses this night."

A look of disappointment momentarily crossed the boy's features. "But I can fight," he reminded Bright Sky, gesturing with his small bow and a quiver of arrows.

"And so you can, but not tonight," Bright Sky said. "A warrior does whatever is necessary to help the people. Sometimes he fights and sometimes he does other things."

"Such as watch the horses?"

Bright Sky smiled and nodded. "That shall be your job tonight, my little warrior, and perhaps tomorrow night as well. Will I be able to depend on you?"

The boy nodded and Bright Sky gripped his shoulder. "Tell Stone Bear you will watch the horses this night."

Little Wolf grinned broadly and dashed off to prepare for his assignment. Bright Sky smiled, remembering how it was with small boys, wishing it was still that way with old men. He walked on through the camp seeking Stone Bear and finally located him at the far end of the camp.

"I feel safe in this place," Bright Sky said, "but warriors should be out there watching."

"We have scouts out," Stone Bear agreed. "They will let us know if anything is wrong."

"I hope so," Bright Sky said. "I keep remembering the Firehole River."

"We will not let it happen again."

"Good," Bright Sky said, feeling reassured. He walked back through the camp, turning finally into his own lodge. Swan had prepared a fire and small supper. He ate quickly, barely tasting the food. He was troubled by the fact that Marcus Cavanaugh's soldiers had not been seen by the scouts lately. It was unlike Marcus to give up, which meant his old friend was still out there somewhere.

He set his bowl of food down, pondering the situation. Perhaps they should move now? Marcus would never expect them to move at night. On the other hand, his people were exhausted and needed rest. He decided he would have to trust in the vigilance of Stone Bear's warriors.

Swan sat down across from him. "You should feel happy that we are almost in the Grandmother Land."

Bright Sky nodded. "I do. But I also fear because we are not there yet, and my worry is that the soldiers will catch us before we are."

She smiled. "Leaders are supposed to worry. That is why they are leaders." She came and knelt next to him, rubbing the back of his neck. "It is also important for leaders to rest," she reminded him. "You have slept little the last few days. Lay down now and sleep."

He nodded. "You are right. Perhaps I should sleep for just a short time. Be sure to awaken me if anything happens."

Swan smiled as he closed his eyes. "I will call you," she said, but he was already asleep.

Bright Sky awoke refreshed. He stepped outside with a glorious new day flooding across the eastern sky. Behind him the looming presence of Horsetooth Mountain was dark and obdurate, waiting for daylight to illuminate its craggy face and timbered, boulder-strewn slopes.

Rising nearly a thousand feet from the plains, the towering peak dominated the surrounding countryside for miles. The Sioux, Bright Sky knew, revered Horse-tooth Mountain as a sacred place.

Plains carpeted with buffalo grass rose to low hills and buttes that fanned out from the great mountain in all directions. A small stream wound sluggishly along the southern apron of the mountain, while the larger Upper Milkweed River cut through the surrounding buttes a mile and a half to the east.

Bright Sky found the dawn cold as he walked silently through the still sleeping camp, feeling glad to have a blanket along, which he drew closer around his shoulders. He stepped across the small stream, noting the ice that had formed on its surface.

He climbed steadily up the slope of the great mountain, weaving his way through the silent stands of cedar, pausing occasionally to catch his breath. Once he startled a doe and fawn feeding and admired their symmetry as they bounded down the slope and out of sight.

Some distance up the slope he discovered what he had hoped to find, a rocky outcrop that afforded a long view of the surrounding country. To the south and north the land was bathed in rapidly fading darkness, its features still largely indistinct, while to the east, the spreading orange dawn gained quickly in intensity.

Below the camp stirred to life. Closing his eyes he breathed deeply and asked the spirit of the mountain to fill him with the wisdom he needed to be a good leader. He thought of his people's desperate needs. The blankets they captured at Antelope Island had helped greatly, but little food was left and no buffalo had been seen at all for some time. Hunters had managed to kill a few antelope, but that meat did not go far among so many.

Where were the soldiers? He wanted desperately to believe they had given up, yet in his heart he sensed that was not likely. If Raven were still here, Michael Bright Sky would not have needed to concern himself so much with the soldiers. And as he thought again of his dead brother, Bright Sky was overcome by the terrible sense of loss and great emptiness within him. It was as though part of him had died with Raven.

The specter of Death had been his silent companion these past days. Bright Sky knew him well. He never spoke and Bright Sky did not see his face clearly. It possessed no definition, no form, yet it was there, tangible and real. Just this morning, as he descended the mountain path, Bright Sky saw Death standing at the burial platforms outside the camp.

The platforms contained two more of their band. One was an old man who had died of hunger and exhaustion, while the other was that of a young warrior who had died of a wound. The specter seemed to be gesturing to him, but Bright Sky held up his hand.

"Sometimes you are tempting," he said. "But I cannot go with you yet. You must come for me another time." And with that the specter faded away.

Bright Sky turned and walked back to his lodge, content with the fact that his people were safe for the moment, and the Grandmother Land was only two sleeps away. They would rest here another day, then finish their journey.

It was late afternoon when Marcus and his party rejoined the regiment. Over supper, John Brandt reported that nothing of significance had occurred during their absence, except that Captain Lemaster had become testier than normal.

Marcus looked at his bearded young adjutant and nodded understandingly. "Been a problem, John?"

Brandt shrugged. "I don't think so, Colonel, but it's something you ought to be aware of."

"I appreciate your bringing it to my attention."

"Did you get everything worked out with Colonel Norris?" Brandt asked.

Marcus nodded. "I think so."

"When do we move?"

"Tomorrow," Marcus answered, briefly reviewing the plan he and Norris had agreed to. "Officers call in thirty minutes. I want to go over the details and issue assignments."

Half an hour later the officers were seated or standing around a warming fire. The day itself had been clear and pleasant. Overhead now, a full moon was impressive in its luminance.

"The Eleventh," Marcus explained, "will approach from the south. We'll make camp tomorrow behind this divide." He pointed on the map to a low range of hills half a mile from the base of Horsetooth Mountain. "We'll attack at first light on the 24th. Norris will start things off with a salvo from his howitzer and that will be our signal to move in. Any questions so far?"

Marcus glanced around the circle of faces. There were no questions, so he continued.

"I'll make final command assignments after we reach the divide. For now, the two-battalion arrangement will remain in place. The pack train and dismounted companies will move out at four a.m., followed by the mounted troops at six, with Captain Foster's battalion in the lead."

"What about the horse herd, Colonel?"

Marcus shook his head. "I'll make that assignment when we reach the divide. We're not exactly sure where the horse herd is. Might be closer to Norris' end of things."

"Seems to me a good scout ought to know where the horse herd is located," a grumbling Stephen Lemaster said as the council broke up.

The remark caught Simon Oliver as he was leaving and brought him up short. Turning, he walked over to Lemaster. "Maybe you'd like to explain that, Captain."

Stephen Lemaster shrugged. "Simple. I said I thought our scout should be able to tell us where the horse herd is located. Maybe you can explain to me why we don't know, Mr. Oliver." He said it flat enough so there was no mistaking the accusation.

Two of the officers who had been among the last to leave heard the remarks and paused to glance over at the two men. Marcus was talking to Brandt, but the exchange caught his attention, too. He looked up just in time to see Simon drive his fist into Lemaster's face, knocking the captain against the trunk of a tree.

Stunned, Lemaster recovered his composure, shook his head and came at the scout. Taller by a couple of inches and heavier by thirty pounds, Lemaster swung a right hand that caught the scout on the side of the head, dropping him to the gound.

"That's enough," Marcus ordered, rushing up to separate the two men. "Captain, get back to your company. Simon, take a walk and cool down."

The scout got to his feet, shaking his head. "Sorry, Marcus. That fool opened his mouth once too often to suit me. Throws a mean punch though, I'll give him that."

Marcus looked at the other officers who had witnessed the fight. "I trust you gentlemen have your commands to prepare for tomorrow," he suggested curtly.

They saluted and walked off.

"I wouldn't take Lemaster's remarks, whatever they

were, too seriously," Marcus said. "He's edgy, that's all."

"We're all edgy, Marcus," the scout pointed out. "But I allow maybe he's got it worse'n the rest of us. See you in the morning, Marcus." He put on his hat and strode off into the darkness.

As with the regular infantry in the field, the dismounted troopers of the Eleventh Cavalry were up and swinging into the day's march in the bone-chilling four a.m. blackness. Behind them came the pack train with it's dwindling stock of supplies.

Their mounted comrades would not be in the saddle for another two hours, which prompted some of the converted foot soldiers to grumble at their misfortune. Come the end of the day, however, the foot sloggers would be resting in camp while the horse soldiers were busy caring for their mounts.

By full sunrise the regiment was well into the rhythm of the march and moving steadily through a clear, cool day. Somewhere around mid-morning, the horsemen moved into the lead, taking the jeers from their comrades on foot and returning their own brand. Marcus smiled as he listened. It was a healthy sign of good spirit.

They nooned early as Marcus wanted to give the men a last opportunity to build coffee fires before the attack. No fires would be permitted beyond this point.

"Enjoy it, gentlemen," Marcus said, lifting his tin of hot coffee. No more 'til after the attack."

"Probably academic," Lieutenant Brandt pointed out, "since we're about at the end of the supply, anyway."

"Maybe Colonel Maynard Norris will offer to share some of his stock with us," Simon observed, producing chuckles all around.

"Simon," Marcus said. "I think it's time for a little reconaissance."

"The horse herd, Marcus?"

Marcus nodded. "And anything else, generally, that we ought to know about. You want some company?"

"Couple or three ought to be enough, in case we need to get some word back to you in a hurry. Hayes and Turley from C be as good as any."

"See he gets them, will you, Lieutenant," Marcus said to Brandt.

The afternoon was waning when they reached the divide. Patrols had worked the country throughout the afternoon. Marcus felt secure that their presence in the area was unknown.

A pastel sunset spread across the western horizon behind them. Simon and his two men returned shortly after dark. He reported that the Nez Perce camp seemed unaware of their presence, although scouts were out and about.

"Horse herd is on this end of the camp, Marcus," he pointed out, sketching a crude map in the dirt. "There's a kind of box canyon behind 'em, which ought to make it easy to round up the critters. I suspect it's why the Nez Perce put 'em there to begin with."

An hour later, Marcus had the officers together for their final briefing.

"The horse herd is on our end of the camp," he explained. "So I'm going to assume the responsibility for it. Foster, you will assign one of your two companies the job of capturing the horses. Your remaining company will have the responsibility of containing any Nez Perce retreat in this direction. Clear?"

Pat Foster nodded.

"Norris will have to assume responsibility for any Nez Perce retreat to the east," Marcus added. "Captain

157

Lemaster, your battalion will strike the camp head-on. You will go in with two companies and hold one in reserve. Let's try and remember, gentlemen, this is not a turkey shoot. Our job is to return the Nez Perce to their reservation alive. I don't want another Sand Creek. Is that clear?"

"Or another Little Big Horn?" Lemaster asked. Marcus grinned. "No, Captain, I'd prefer to avoid that, too."

The response produced a few laughs. Snow was just beginning to swirl as the meeting dispersed.

"Very well, gentlemen. If there are no further questions, see to your companies and get some sleep."

Chapter Eighteen

The council fire burned strongly and warmed the lodge nicely, making the gathering of elders comfortable by driving back the chill that made its presence felt with the disappearance of the sun each afternoon.

"The people cannot go on like this much longer," one member pointed out, producing nods of agreement around the circle.

"The old ones . . . "

"Such as you, Hump?" another said, drawing laughs from the group.

"Such as all of us," the one called Hump replied. "All of us old ones and the children," he went on. "If we do not reach the Grandmother Land soon, we will have no choice but to surrender to the soldiers."

"I will never be that tired!" said another defiantly.

"We are not far from the Grandmother Land," another pointed out. "Two sleeps at most. Can we not last that much longer?"

"For some, even two days is too much," Hump replied.

Bright Sky listened attentively, addressing the group only after each had spoken his mind.

"It is true the people are weary, and we have not much food left. It is also true that all of us have suffered and many have died so that we might reach the Grandmother Land. Their lives must not be wasted. We must travel soon for there is little time left."

Bright Sky looked at sober expressions as the elders pondered his words. "I say this, too," he went on. "Let us send two warriors to the Grandmother Land to find the Sioux and ask them for help. Surely they will not turn us down."

With nods of affirmation, the council approved the idea.

"Who will go?" Hump asked.

Several nominations were made, but no consensus was reached.

"We should let Stone Bear choose the warriors," Bright Sky said softly.

"Yes, it is his right," Hump agreed, and the others nodded.

After the council had dispersed, Bright Sky remained in front of the fire, idly feeding small pieces of fresh wood to the hungry flames. Behind him, Swan moved about, readying their bed for the night.

"I must walk for a while and clear my head," he said, getting to his feet.

Swan looked at him with some concern, started to say something and thought better of it.

Bright Sky stepped out into the darkness, feeling the light feathery touch of the falling snow. He drew the blanket up closely around his neck and shoulders and walked through the camp, striding slowly, thoughtfully.

He walked on through the thick flakes of snow to the edge of the camp, pausing to look across the small meandering stream toward the land that rose slightly upward from the stream, to the horse herd, their rumps turned in the direction of the approaching snow storm.

The snow was falling harder, but if it made their journey more difficult, it would also make it harder for Marcus Cavanaugh and his soldiers.

Turning, Michael Bright Sky walked back through the camp, noting a single dog that came scampering out to snap at him. In the old days, there were many dogs, but now they were mostly gone, killed along the way and consigned to some family's meager stew pot.

Swan was asleep when he returned to the lodge. Quietly he eased his tired body in beside her, allowing himself the luxury of dwelling on the prospect of the Grandmother Land where they could relax and live again without fear of soldiers coming after them.

Colonel Maynard Norris sat on his black gelding, his hands crossed on the saddle in front of him, watching his command file into bivouac. He was proud of this regiment. The Twenty-ninth Infantry was, in his view, the finest in the service. Having assumed command of the regiment three years ago, he had molded and shaped it until it was an extension of himself.

Eight of the regiment's complement of ten companies had joined him for this campaign, the remaining two being left behind as garrison troops. The eight companies numbered nearly four hundred officers and men, supported by three companies, one hundred and fifty troopers, of the Sixteenth Cavalry, together with a contingent of eighty Crow Indian scouts. In total, Norris' column numbered more than six hundred men, plus a mountain howitzer and supply train of thirty wagons.

Fresh, trim and well supplied, it was a strong, healthy force, particularly when compared to the field-worn troopers of Marcus Cavanaugh's Eleventh Cavalry.

"Officers call soon as all are on hand, Captain," he said, turning slightly to address his adjutant, a clean-shaven man of thirty. The captain nodded, tossed a salute at Norris and headed down off the low ridge to make the necessary arrangements.

Within half an hour, Norris' tent had been erected and the Colonel was inside peering intently over a detailed map of the area. Much was shown as little more than blank space and *terra incognita*. Behind him a Sibley stove was beginning to radiate warmth.

Producing a cigar from his breast pocket, Norris lit it and drew thoughtfully, expelling the smoke in a long steady stream. Tomorrow's attack would require some aggressive action on his part if the Twenty-ninth was to benefit from this campaign. And of course it wouldn't hurt his own chances for a brigadier's star either. There would be a vacancy next year and something solid at Horsetooth Mountain would certainly enhance his own position.

Under no circumstances of course would personal gain be placed above the importance of the assignment itself. He recognized as well that Marcus Cavanaugh and the Eleventh Cavalry had been in the field for weeks now and had earned the right to lead the final attack. But God was on the side of the heaviest battalions, he reasoned. And if the important thing was the success of the attack, then individual rights were secondary. Having thus satisfied himself as to what his command must do, Maynard Norris returned to his scrutiny of the map.

Later, when his commanders had assembled, Norris set forth his plan.

"This is a roundup, gentlemen. It is our job, along with Colonel Cavanaugh's command, to see that Bright Sky and his Nez Perce are returned to their reservation. Of course, in actions such as this someone is going to get hurt, but the idea is to minimize casualties as much as possible. That's straight from Washington."

The remark raised a few smiles.

"We'll fire a couple of air bursts with the howitzer to get things started. That ought to rattle the Nez Perce. Major Smythe, your battalion of the Twenty-ninth will drive into the camp from this side. Your battalion will be in reserve, Stanford. Major Tyree, the cavalry's job will be to cut off any escape."

"We understand Colonel Cavanaugh's Eleventh Cavalry will be joining in the attack, Colonel."

Norris nodded. "Yes. Colonel Cavanaugh will be hitting the camp from the south." He pointed to the general area of Marcus' attack. "The first shot from the howitzer will be Colonel Cavanaugh's signal to attack." Someone in the group coughed. Norris paused, visibly annoyed.

"With respect to cooperation, gentlemen, I can only say you will have to let your tactical decisions be governed by circumstances as you find them. It would be unfair and unrealistic of me to burden you with precise instructions regarding Colonel Cavanaugh's plan of attack. I know only his general direction of attack as he knows mine."

He paused, letting his eyes roam around the gathered knot of officers. "Well then, gentlemen, let's do it for the old Twenty- ninth, eh? Oh! And of course to our comrades of the saddle from the Sixteenth Regiment, we welcome your participation."

When the officers had left, Norris ran the planned sequence of events through his mind one last time. Finally satisfied that nothing had been omitted, he lit a cigar. Producing a small flask from his saddlebags, he raised it in a silent toast and drank sparingly. Replacing the flask, he stepped to the entrance of his tent and watched the spiraling snow flakes layering the country with a mantle of white.

Chapter Nineteen

For the men of Colonel Marcus Cavanaugh's Eleventh Regiment of Cavalry, the day began at three a.m. when duty sergeants were awakened by sentries. They in turn woke the men of their respective companies. The soldiers grumbled and cursed over their misfortune at having to rise at such an ungodly hour, especially since it meant moving through three inches of fresh snow and finger-numbing cold. If anything good could be said of the weather, it was that the snow had stopped falling, though to the men of the Eleventh Cavalry it was a moot point.

The troopers stumbled through the bivouac area, relieving themselves wherever it proved convenient before proceeding with such details as checking weapons, saddling horses and general preparation for the day's work. In the morning darkness, punctured only by the dull glow of Captain Pat Foster's pipe, Marcus quickly reviewed the command assignments with Foster and Lemaster.

"Remember," he reminded both men, "our signal will be firing from the northeast, which will be Norris' scouts."

The two officers nodded and Marcus continued.

"Simon, Lieutenant Brandt, I want you with me. We'll be in the general vicinity of the horse herd, at least to start with. And I don't have to remind you of the need for a silent approach. Unless there are any questions, let's get on with it."

Each man turned and moved through the cold darkness to his respective command, his foot-falls crunching in the freshly fallen snow.

Half an hour later they were in the saddle and moving. Foster's battalion led the way, followed by Lemaster and the dismounted companies. Accompanied by Simon and Lieutenant Brandt, Marcus rode point with Pat Foster and G Company.

Behind them, the hooves of nearly three hundred shod horses thudded softly on the frozen ground. All loose equipment had been secured to prevent rattling, so that the column moved through the cold tomb of black dawn with surprising quiet.

Cresting the divide, they moved down the slope. The Nez Perce camp lay less than a mile ahead, just beyond a series of low, jagged hills. Horsetooth Mountain loomed, forebidding and omnipotent, like some great God of the Plains awaiting the drama about to be acted out on the stage at his feet.

In the slowly graying dawn, the column halted at the edge of the low lying hills. With G Company in tow, Marcus, Simon and Pat Foster rode along the apron of the hills to where they tapered down to meet the floor of the plain. From here they could barely make out the horse herd.

"Questions, Captain?"

"None, Colonel. We'll be ready when Norris is."

"Good luck, Pat," Marcus said, extending his hand. "See you in the village."

"Right, sir."

By the time he returned to the regiment, Lemaster had positioned his three-company battalion for its attack on the flank of the village. The remaining company of Foster's battalion took positions along the crest of the hills, from where it would be able to turn back any Nez Perce who tried to escape in that direction. The pack train and dismounted companies had not arrived as yet and were designated as the regimental reserve to be used where needed.

With each unit in its assigned position, there was nothing further to do but wait for the signal from Norris' scouts. Marcus glanced at the eastern horizon where a ribbon of color was just beginning to emerge. Around him, the horses stomped and snorted, expelling their breaths in the frosty air.

Wrapped in a huge buffalo coat, only Maynard Norris' feet were cold. He watched the mountain howitzer being moved by human strength only, into position on the crest of a small hill overlooking the Nez Perce camp. The route of the field piece could be followed by tracing the twin ribbons of wheel track up the snow-covered hillside from the bivouac area below.

Maynard Norris had a special place in his heart for artillery as a result of time spent in the artillery branch of the service during the early months of the Civil War. It wasn't all nostalgia though. On the frontier he had seen the psychological effect that field pieces had on Indians, so wherever possible he made it a point to have at least one on his campaigns.

This morning the gunners grunted and groaned,

slipped and slid as they pushed and pulled the howitzer up the slick, snow-covered hillside. It took him back to Bolger's Spring, Kentucky, in that first winter of the Civil War—a haunting setting that was recalled with near-perfect clarity—a young second lieutenant of artillery, he tasted combat for the first time. On that occasion he had been one of two men pushing a field piece up a steep slope, the others in the battery having been killed by Confederate fire.

The inky blackness of night still prevailed, but it was beginning to weaken. He glanced around with a practiced eye.

"Thirty minutes at the outside," he said, addressing his adjutant. "All units in place?"

"Yes, sir."

Presently, an officer walked over and reported that the howitzer was ready.

"Very well," Norris said. "Stand by, Lieutenant."

The lieutenant saluted and returned to the gun.

Norris walked over to the edge of the hill, past the silent gun and down the forward slope a short distance to a large rock outcropping. Stepping out on the rock he stared down into the still darkened valley, barely able to discern the shapes of the Nez Perce lodges.

Down there, he thought, lay his brigadier's star, and he was determined that it would not be denied. He thought, too, of the sobriquet, "Mad Maynard" and smiled, for he cherished the public persona, believing that advancement in this man's army stood in direct proportion to one's legend.

At length he turned and walked back to the crest of the hill to his waiting adjutant. Glancing east, he noted the thin wisp of orange beginning to emerge on the horizon, and nodded to his adjutant, who in turn signaled the howitzer crews. A moment later the arriving dawn was ushered in by successive blasts from the two field pieces.

Little Wolf awoke feeling the cold that had penetrated his family's makeshift lodge. Last night's fire had not provided much warmth, for the makeshift lodge was not designed to retain heat the way their old lodge did. Still, it was better than no lodge at all. He looked around at the sleeping forms of his mother and grandfather and roused himself quietly so as not to waken them.

Taking his blanket, bow and quiver of arrows, he stepped outside into a world of white freshness, shuddering as he wrapped the blanket around his shoulders. Other than the tracks of a single rabbit, his were the only marks in the mantle of new snow. It pleased him to be the first of the village awake. And he took special pride in the fact that Bright Sky had asked him to help guard the horse herd. He made a vow to honor his father's memory by proving equal to the responsibility.

He trudged quickly through the fresh snow toward the horse herd to relieve the night guard. Soldiers liked to attack at dawn, he had heard Bright Sky say, and with that in mind he reasoned it might be helpful for him to be on hand early.

When he reached the herd, the night guard was glad for the company. As far as Little Wolf was concerned, however, this was not a social call. Accordingly, after a courteous exchange of pleasantries with the guard, he decided a tour of inspection was in order and headed for the far end of the herd to begin there. The guard smiled to himself and shrugged, watching the boy disappear into the grayness of the nascent dawn.

As he moved through the herd Little Wolf imagined that the horses seemed nervous and skittish, but the guard laughed when he mentioned it. Little Wolf had been embarrassed to press the point. And since there was really no evidence to support his feeling, he wondered if perhaps it was his imagination as the guard suggested. Nevertheless, the notion persisted, causing him to remain especially alert as he continued on his rounds.

At the far end of the herd, near where a low range of hills ended, he thought he detected movement, but it was still too dark for him to be sure. Straining to see across the intervening two hundred yards, he finally concluded his eyes were deceiving him.

He had just turned to walk back through the herd, noting the sliver of orange in the east, when he heard a loud boom that was much like the thunder. It was followed by a second boom a moment later. Hard on the heels of that he heard the firing of rifles from the same direction. From behind him, more rifle fire sounded closer and louder. He swung around, and in the dim light saw a body of riders thundering down on him.

Speechless at first, he finally found his voice. Discarding his blanket, he took off on a dead run for the village, shouting, "Soldiers! Soldiers!"

When the sound of Norris' howitzer boomed through the gray dawn, Marcus turned to Simon Oliver and John Brandt.

"Well, gentlemen. Shall we be off?"

Swinging into his saddle, he nodded to Stephen Lemaster.

"Captain . . . "

For once, the abrasive Lemaster found it unnecessary to respond with anything but compliance. Cold and keyed-up, the troopers of his battalion welcomed the opportunity to restore some circulation and responded with exuberance.

170

With F Company in the middle, flanked on the left by A, and B on the right, Lemaster's battalion mounted the ridge and swept down across the two hundred yards separating them from the end of the Nez Perce camp. To the south, their comrades in G Company descended down on the horse herd. Marcus rode next to Brandt and a surprisingly boisterous Simon Oliver, accompanying the lead elements of Lemaster's battalion.

As they thundered across the snow covered ground toward the village, Marcus felt caught up in the heady exuberance of the charge, triggering a rush of memories from nearly twenty years in the past when he had ridden down the Shenandoah with Sheridan.

The ground beneath them swept past quickly, and as they approached the Nez Perce camp he could see figures stumbling out of lodges, swarming helter-skelter, seeking shelter from the oncoming troopers. Cavanaugh was reminded of a similar morning a few weeks earlier at the Firehole River, and of the disaster it had turned out to be. The difference this time was that whatever else he was, Maynard Norris was no Israel Damon.

A few scattered shots began to greet the invaders as warriors, recovering from their surprise, sought out positions from which to fight back. Some Indians were felled almost immediately as they emerged from their lodges, blood staining the snow beneath limp bodies. Here and there a warrior managed to crawl or limp away from where he'd fallen, in search of safety.

Women, children and old people moved frantically back through the camp as quickly as their age and physical condition permitted, seeking the shelter of ravines on the far side of the small stream.

Colt in hand, Marcus hauled his mount in at the near end of the camp, pausing to survey the situation, using his left hand to control the excited animal. Visibility was improving quickly as the day grew brighter. To the south, it appeared that Pat Foster had the horse herd well in hand, while Lemaster's battalion was driving into the flank of the village, meeting no organized resistance, although return fire from the Nez Perce was beginning to pick up.

Away to the east, around a bend of the stream where the remainder of the camp was not visible, Marcus heard the staccato fire of Norris' troops advancing from the east. Caught between two advancing forces, the Nez Perce had little chance of turning the tide.

The sound of scattered shots roused Bright Sky from an uneasy sleep. The gunfire was like the recurring nightmare of the Firehole River. He had not wanted to believe it could happen again, and yet that was exactly what was taking place here this morning.

He rushed outside, noted the chaos that was building as the attack intensified. Realizing he had no weapon, he ducked back in the lodge, grabbed his Winchester and paused long enough to exhort Swan to leave quickly.

"Some are taking cover across the stream. You must hurry."

Swan snatched her blanket and headed out. "Take care of yourself," she admonished him. He nodded. "You must do the same."

Outside, Bright Sky spotted a small cluster of warriors who had taken a position behind a small knoll. He moved over to join them. Stone Bear was one of the group. Barely clothed, the five warriors lay in the snow, using the protection of the knoll to return fire at the advancing troops.

"Not good," Bright Sky muttered, glancing around

at the camp, where a few lodges at the far end of the camp had already been set afire by Lemaster's advancing troops.

Stone Bear nodded. "Yes, but not as bad as it might be," he pointed out. "That boy, Little Wolf?"

Bright Sky nodded.

"He went out to the horse herd very early and gave the alarm when the soldiers began their attack. His warning gave some of us a chance to fight back."

Bright Sky smiled. The boy deserved their best effort. As he scanned the surrounding area, Bright Sky noted several small pockets of resistance much like their own.

One of them was positioned behind a tumbled tangle of overturned cottonwoods fifty yards ahead.

"We must join them, somehow," Bright Sky said to the others. "We will be stronger if we fight together."

Bright Sky led the way. The new location gave them an effective position from which to pour critical fire into the left flank of the soldiers.

"We can hold them here for a while but not long," Bright Sky said. "They come at us from both ends and we have not strength enough to fight in two places. Our only chance is to get to the gullies and ravines where our families are. We must try and bring all of the warriors together there." He paused to gesture toward the far side of the stream. "I will take three of these men with me, you move the others across the stream. I will join you there."

Stone Bear nodded in agreement, collected the remaining warriors and moved toward the designated area. From here they continued their fire on the troopers, who were now advancing slowly on foot.

Within an hour, Bright Sky had joined them with another group and through the course of the morning their numbers swelled as more and more warriors arrived, singly and in small groups. As their numbers grew, so did the volume of return fire they were able to concentrate against the advancing troops.

"Uncomfortable" was how Lemaster had put it, and he might have added "downright disturbing."

Soldiers, who had been advancing steadily from both directions, were slowed at first, then stymied altogether, as the Nez Perce resistance began to stiffen. Compelled to exchange fire with the villagers on unequal terms now—they had less cover than the defenders—the troops began to sustain heavier casualties than expected.

In an effort to overpower the Nez Perce, Marcus ordered the dismounted companies to move forward and add the strength of their fire to the others. It gave Marcus just over two hundred effectives, not counting Foster's command. He had to deal with some three hundred Nez Perce warriors, who were also forced to contend with the pressure exerted by Norris' command advancing from the east.

One bright spot was Brandt's report that Pat Foster had the horse herd fully under control and was driving it back to the troops' assembly area back of the divide. Marcus sent a courier with orders for Foster to leave a platoon as herd guard and rejoin them with the rest of his company.

The day itself had slowly warmed as the sun moved steadily across the pale blue, cloudless sky. Gradually it melted much of the snow, leaving soggy earth beneath. The exchange of fire persisted into the early afternoon. On three occasions, Marcus sent probes forward in an effort to penetrate the Nez Perce position, but each time they were forced to retire.

174

By mid-afternoon, Marcus and Brandt rode east to confer with Norris, whom they discovered to be no less frustrated over the stubbornness of the Nez Perce resistance.

"Marcus," Norris began. "I've purposely avoided using the howitzers because of the women and children. But we may not have any choice."

"Colonel, I think we may have more of a choice than Bright Sky."

"Eh, how's that, Marcus?"

"Simple, really," Marcus explained. "He's got nowhere to go and virtually nothing to live on where he is. Maybe a warrior or two could escape, but there's no way that whole camp is going to make it out of there without our permission."

"Hmmf," Norris snorted. "Suppose you're right, Marcus, but so what?"

"We just sit tight, Colonel and wait for Bright Sky to come to us, which I believe he'll do. When that happens it's all over. The Nez Perce are forced to surrender. There are no further casualties and Washington's satisfied."

Maynard Norris nodded, jamming a cigar into his mouth. "I agree, Marcus. We wait."

Chapter Twenty

The shallow warmth of the day faded quickly as the sun set beyond the lip of the western horizon. The falling temperature added to the growing discomfort of the Nez Perce, who huddled together in the ravines around small fires.

Beyond the stream another lodge burst into flame as soldiers put torches to the camp, destroying the remaining possessions of the Indians. It had been Norris' idea to burn the village, believing it might provide incentive for the Nez Perce to surrender. Marcus had argued against it. The Nez Perce would need shelter when they finally did surrender, and it made no sense to destroy what little food remained since that meant the Nez Perce would have to be fed from the troops' supply. Norris, however, felt it necessary to impose his own peculiar stamp on this campaign. The order stood.

Bright Sky walked among the people. For the first time since their odyssey had begun he felt a sense of complete failure and it weighed heavily on him. With the arrival of darkness, the gunfire had tapered off. Now only an occasinal shot shattered the cold darkness.

Two of the warriors brought the body of Little Wolf to him, just as they had brought the body of Raven. Despite being wounded, they said, he had continued to fight the soldiers who came to take the horses. Finally, according to the night guard who had managed to survive, the boy had been struck down by a second bullet.

When Bright Sky recognized the inert form of Little Wolf he felt a profound anguish. As he moved among the people, drawing the worn blanket closer about his shoulders, he passed an old man and woman huddled over a small fire. The man had been a warrior of some renown as a young man. Now in advanced years, it was remarkable that he had survived the journey thus far. The woman was wrapped in a blanket but the old warrior had none. Bright Sky removed his own and placed it around the old man's shoulders.

"Warm yourself with this, old man. I may have need for your skills as a warrior."

The old man looked up at him with a toothless grin. "I will be ready," he said proudly.

The night deepened, drawing back a curtain on the jeweled splendor of the heavens, cold and aloof, yet stunningly beautiful. Bright Sky continued his rounds, encouraging his people to be courageous for just a while longer, uttering words that sounded hollow to him even as he spoke them.

Returning to his own small fire, he seated himself beside Swan, who allowed him a few moments of silence before offering him a small cup of soup made from water and a few scraps of dried buffalo meat. He sipped it, reluctantly at first, then willingly as the hot liquid funneled through his chilled bones.

"What will you do?" Swan asked at length.

He looked at her and shook his head. "I don't know. We have not heard from our warriors who went to see the Sioux. Perhaps they will return soon with good news." His voice trailed off as he stared into the flames and she pursued the issue no further.

How long he dozed, there in front of the fire, he didn't know, but when his head dropped once too sharply, it roused him to wakefulness and a tingling sensation in his foot. He looked about, rubbed his eyes and stood up, stamping his sleep-numbed foot to life.

Around him mostly inert forms were lying or sitting, trying as best they could to wade through the night and its cold. Swan stirred when he arose and got up to join him.

"It is too cold to sleep," she declared, rubbing her arms.

He nodded and reached down to grab a handful of small branches, which he dropped over the glowing orange coals. Crouching down he blew softly on the coals. Little tongues of flame grew to life, licking the fresh branches.

Overhead, a brilliant silver disk of moon was poised over the looming hulk of Horsetooth Mountain, bathing the country below in a pale, luminous light.

On the far side of the stream he could occasionally make out the moving shape of some soldier, and he found himself wondering whether it might be Marcus. It was just as cold where the soldiers were, he told himself, but then he realized that the soldiers had warm clothes and were mostly young warriors. Here, many were very young or very old, and few had warm clothing.

Placing more wood on the fire, he eased himself down to ponder their situation. When light returned, the fighting would resume. Fire from the warriors' guns would hit some of the soldiers, but there would also be more casualties among the people. Food and ammunition was also running low. They could not hold out here much longer, and he suspected Marcus Cavanaugh knew that as well. The only remaining hope it seemed was help from the Sioux.

The night was thinning to gray when he felt a hand on his shoulder, shaking him gently. He turned to see Stone Bear standing there with the two emissaries that had been sent to ask for help from the Sioux.

He motioned them to sit, adding the last few pieces of wood from his supply to the mound of orange coals, fanning them to life while the three warriors waited patiently.

"Do you bring good news?" he inquired at length.

The pair glanced briefly at each other, shaking their heads.

"The Sioux understand our problems, but they can do nothing to help without risk to themselves. They fear that by helping us the Mounted Police may order them to leave the Grandmother Country."

"Besides," his companion added, "they have very little themselves."

Bright Sky nodded. "It is as I feared it might be." His voice trailed off and his shoulders sank in defeat. "Tell the elders we must meet," he told Stone Bear. "The time has come."

The first color of the new day tinged the horizon, steadily gaining in strength. As soon as conditions brightened sufficiently to pick out a target, the troops all along the line resumed firing, and in turn drew fire from the Nez Perce.

From his makeshift command post at the base of a large uprooted cottonwood stump, Marcus surveyed the Nez Perce position. A momentary flash of orange deep in the woods indicated the position of an Indian rifleman. Along his own line, officers shouted and non-coms exhorted the troopers to keep down and pick their targets. The troops offered little profile for the Nez Perce to fire at.

By mid-morning both commands had moved detachments forward against the Nez Perce flanks, pinching them back and giving the troops an opportunity to deliver fire against the defenders from an enfilading position. Additionally, Maynard Norris' scouts worked their way around behind the Nez Perce right, applying further pressure from that direction.

Marcus was moving laterally along the line toward Lemaster when a Nez Perce bullet drove into his left shoulder and spun him around. Falling to one knee, he grabbed the shoulder, attempted to rise and dropped back down. Hands were helping him to his feet.

"Better get you to the surgeon, Colonel," Lieutenant Brandt said calmly, and called for an orderly.

Marcus shook his head to clear the blurred vision. "Tell Lemaster to take command for the time being, John."

Brandt nodded. "I'll attend to it, sir."

Half an hour later, the surgeon finished the last of his bandaging. "You're fortunate, Colonel, in that the bullet passed through cleanly. You'll be sore for a while, but nothing that shouldn't heal."

"Thanks, Doc," Marcus said, getting to his feet. The ground began to spin and he was forced to grab the surgeon's arm to keep from falling. Now that the shock was wearing off, the full impact of the pain was beginning to set in.

"You might try resting for a while, Colonel, though

I should know better than to even suggest such a thing."

"Your concern is appreciated, Doc. I'll be fine," Marcus reassured him. He headed back to his command post, meeting Lemaster and Brandt on the way.

"How's the shoulder, Colonel?" Lemaster asked.

"Clean wound. I'll be fine," Marcus said.

"This may be what we've been waiting for, Colonel. Two Nez Perce have come forward with a white flag. It's a bit on the dirty gray side, but close enough to tell that's what it is," Brandt said, grinning.

"They're waiting at my company, Colonel."

"Bring then down here, John, and get a message to Norris right away." Marcus eased himself down against a tree stump. "Oh, and issue a cease fire order for now."

"Right, sir." Brandt hastily scribbled out a message for a courier, while Lemaster headed back to his company.

The pain was steady and Cavanaugh felt weak from the loss of blood. Ames handed him a tin of hot coffee, which at least felt good if it accomplished nothing else. He leaned back, feeling suddenly light-headed again, and then there was nothing.

"Colonel! Colonel!"

The voice came to him from a great distance. He opened his eyes to see Lemaster standing in front of him with two haggard Nez Perce warriors. He struggled to his feet.

"You are Marcus Cavanaugh..?"

Marcus nodded. "I am Colonel Cavanaugh."

"Bright Sky has asked us to come to you and say that we are ready to surrender. But he will surrender only to you."

"Tell Bright Sky I will be glad to speak with him, but

there is another officer who must be regarded as head of all the soldiers here."

"I will tell him," the warrior said.

A few wisps of thin clouds streaked the mid-day sky, but the autumn sun shone brightly, warming the cold land. Maynard Norris paced impatiently, chewing on the end of his cigar, now and then glancing toward the Nez Perce positions. Marcus was still seated against the tree stump. Lemaster, Brandt, Norris' adjutant and a pair of reporters stood nearby.

"Damned unfair if you ask me," Norris said. "All this way only to be wounded right at the finish. Oh well, I guess a soldier never knows, eh, Marcus?"

Marcus forced a grin. "Well, this way at least I didn't have to miss anything."

"Excuse me, sir, but I believe the Indians are heading this way," Lieutenant Brandt interrupted.

Getting slowly to his feet, Marcus looked out at the three figures walking slowly but steadily toward them. There was no mistaking mistaking Bright Sky. The man carried himself with such extraordinary dignity, you could spot him even from a distance.

A few moments later, Marcus and Bright Sky were standing face to face. Marcus introduced Norris, then Lemaster and Brandt who stood off to one side. Bright Sky introduced Stone Bear and Horn, the two earlier emissaries.

Norris invited them to sit. "Well, you've given us quite a chase, Bright Sky," he smiled sadly.

The Nez Perce leader studied Maynard Norris for a long moment. "Yes. If only we could have thought of it as a game. But it is not a game, and now my people will die on the reservation."

Maynard Norris cleared his throat. "You are prepared to surrender and return peacefully to your reservation?"

Bright Sky's nod of assent was barely perceptible. "I no longer have a choice. Our food is gone and we have but few remaining bullets for our weapons. The people are suffering. Some are sick, and we have warriors who are wounded."

He paused to look at Marcus. "I am sorry you were wounded, old friend. It is a terrible thing about war that makes a friend fight a friend."

Marcus nodded. "Why, old friend, did you permit this to continue? So many have been hurt!"

Bright Sky looked at Marcus, then off into the distance. "Why, old friend? You left us no choice. If a man surrenders his spirit, what is left, Marcus? Remember the Grizzly Mountains?"

"I remember, old friend," Marcus said. "I remember that time as clearly as I see this moment."

"That was our spirit, Marcus, our will to live. If you take that away there is only death. I have seen Death, Marcus. He wanted me once, but I sent him away and he still waits. We shall fight no more, Marcus Cavanaugh, but we shall never surrender our spirit."

Bright Sky smiled softly and turned back to Norris. "We have come many miles since leaving our homeland. Many who began the journey are no longer with us, even though their spirits have given us strength along the way. But for the sake of the living, we cannot continue. The price is too great. So I offer the surrender of my people, in all matters except spirit, both now and for as long as it remains in my power to pledge."

Eloquent in their simplicity, the words would have broken the heart of Death himself. Even "Mad" Maynard Norris was visibly moved. He glanced briefly at Marcus, then back at the sad, proud face of Bright Sky.

"Ahem. Yes, well . . . " Norris began, clearing his throat. "Marcus, I think you ought to be the one to accept the surrender."

The offer was somewhat out of character for Norris, and it caught Marcus by surprise.

"Very well. I accept, Colonel." Marcus extended his free hand to Bright Sky and felt the firmness of the other's grasp. "Your surrender is accepted, old friend. We will of course provide your people with as much help as we can."

"And I shall personally see that everything possible is done to help you and your people, " Norris added.

Softly, Bright Sky placed a hand on Marcus' shoulder. "I must tell the people that it is over."

When Bright Sky had left, Marcus turned to Norris. "If you will excuse me, Colonel, I'd best be seeing to my command."

"Of course, Colonel. Will you join me for supper this evening?"

"My pleasure," Marcus said before walking off.

Maynard Norris turned to the reporters who had been busy taking notes.

"Two very special men," Norris noted. "And a very special moment, gentlemen. Remember it well."

Norris' adjutant was surprised, for he was unaccustomed to hearing his colonel toss out superlatives about others. This was indeed a special moment in history.

"I was surprised to hear your offer of intercession for the Nez Perce back there, Colonel," the adjutant said, broaching the silence as the two men walked slowly back to their own headquarters.

"How's that? Oh, yes. Well, Captain, you know there's more than one way to a brigadier's star," he said, smiling. "There will soon be much sympathy for the Nez Perce cause in Washington."

The adjutant nodded. He should have known.

Marcus had tried to sleep, but the pain made it impossible, so he had roused himself into a sitting position. After poking at the remains of the fire for a few moments, he was grateful when Ames materialized out of nowhere to assume responsibility for a really first class blaze.

After Marcus, had settled down in front of the blaze, Ames handed him a cup of coffee, then disappeared into the blackness from which he'd emerged.

"Believe I could manage to sweeten that for you a bit," Simon Oliver said, easing down beside Marcus and pouring a healthy portion of whiskey into the steaming coffee. "If that don't make you sleep, Marcus, I reckon nothing will."

Marcus sipped and convulsed slightly as the modified coffee coursed through his insides.

"Potent, Simon."

"Amen, Marcus. Amen." The scout lifted the flask to his lips and drank deeply, coughing once. "I allow we've deserved pleasure these many weeks, Marcus."

"You've been holding out on me, Simon."

"Only for a good cause, Marcus. Tonight."

Marcus grinned and took another swallow, feeling the whiskey's warmth capture his body. The pain in his shoulder seemed a little more bearable. He leaned his head back, having suddenly found the drowsiness that had eluded him earlier.

"I've turned the regiment over to Lemaster, Simon. We're starting back to Casey tomorrow. He could use your help."

"I'll see to it, Marcus. Get some sleep."

When the scout had disappeared into the night, Marcus brought out Elizabeth's letter and reread it, the flames casting shadows across the paper. Now that the campaign was over he found himself thinking again of the East and Elizabeth.

The West he had come to know as a young officer had changed dramatically in his years of service. Buffalo were seldom seen, and the Indians who hunted them were on reservations. The open range was fenced and the country was beginning to see roads and settlements. It was the end of an era for the American West, and Michael Bright Sky's defeat was little more than a brief chapter in that greater epic.

Marcus Cavanaugh smiled with the memory of the last night he had seen Elizabeth. It was the same night he first had word of the the flight of the Nez Perce—the beginning of a long hard journey. He had a furlough coming, and he decided to go east, and call on Elizabeth in New York. It was a comforting thought, and the last thing he remembered before Simon's whiskey brought, finally, the sleep his body craved.